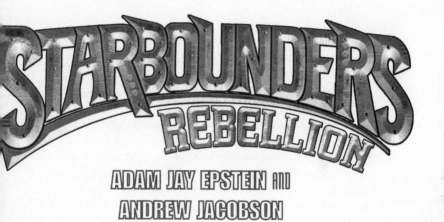

STARBOUNDERS
REBELLION

ADAM JAY EPSTEIN AND
ANDREW JACOBSON

HARPER
An Imprint of HarperCollins*Publishers*

Starbounders #2: Rebellion
Text copyright © 2014 by Adam Jay Epstein and Andrew Jacobson
Illustrations copyright © 2014 by David McClellan

Library of Congress Cataloging-in-Publication Data

Epstein, Adam Jay.
   Rebellion / Adam Jay Epstein & Andrew Jacobson.
      pages   cm. — (Starbounders ; 2)
   Summary: "Four young Starbounder students must once again risk their lives, travel
throughout space, and dismantle an evil conspiracy to save their world"— Provided by
publisher.
   ISBN 978-0-06-212027-4 (hardback)
   [1. Adventure and adventurers—Fiction. 2. Schools—Fiction. 3. Extraterrestrial
beings—Fiction. 4. Life on other planets—Fiction. 5. Space flight—Fiction. 6. Science
fiction.] I. Jacobson, Andrew. II. Title.
PZ7.E72514Reb 2014   2013047724
[Fic]—dc23   CIP
                                                                              AC

14 15 16 17 18   CG/RRDH   10 9 8 7 6 5 4 3 2 1

First Edition

For Andrew, my writing partner.

And Christopher, who introduced me to the most important person in my life.

—A. J. E.

For Scott, my older brother.

Thanks for teaching me everything I know.

—A. J.

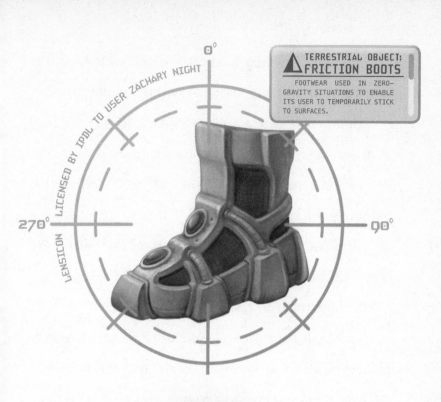

0°

270°

90°

TERRESTRIAL OBJECT:
FRICTION BOOTS
FOOTWEAR USED IN ZERO-
GRAVITY SITUATIONS TO ENABLE
ITS USER TO TEMPORARILY STICK
TO SURFACES.

«ONE»

Zachary's friction boots held fast as he twisted to dodge his opponent's flexible combat stick. Before she swung again, Zachary somersaulted to what looked like an inverted staircase nearby. Zachary and Tai Sunaka were the final two Lightwings competing in the sparring duel, one in a series of contests that would determine the SQ captains for the annual Indigo Starbounder Games. Tai springboarded through the gravity-free environment of the Qube, blocking Zachary's attack with her wrist guard and striking him hard in the thigh as she passed.

"Hey, watch where you swing that thing," Zachary said, wincing from his upside-down perch.

"Less talk, more stick," Tai snapped back, with another lightning-quick hit to his shin. Then to his abdomen. Throat. Face. Zachary tried to brush off each successive blow, but the last one—a brutal strike to his bicep—stung a little more than the rest.

It had only been a few weeks since Zachary's late morphology instructor, Professor Olari, had taken hold of Zachary's arm and burned a strange symbol into his flesh. With his dying breath, Olari had asked Zachary to use the knowledge he had left him to continue what he had started—and, oh yeah, every known galaxy was at risk if Zachary failed.

Upon their return to Indigo 8, a hidden Earth base for Starbounders-in-training, it hadn't taken Zachary's friend Quee long to recognize the symbol on Zachary's arm. It was identical to one on a pair of hacking hands—robotic hands used to disguise a cyber criminal's fingerprints while infiltrating an enemy computer system—she'd taken from a discarded carapace. She'd used the serial number engraved on them to determine that the hands were made in the Exo-Shell factory on the planet of Adranus. Someone there would surely be able to translate the message buried in the symbol; now they just had to figure out a way to get there.

"Ninety seconds remaining." Cerebella, Indigo 8's mainframe computer stated, her voice echoing through the giant glass cube.

Zachary had won his first four sparring duels in the round-robin tournament, and defeating Tai would all but guarantee his spot as one of the captains. But being a captain was the furthest thing from Zachary's mind. Winning was reward enough for him. Unfortunately, in this duel, he was behind on points, so the only way to get the victory was by scoring a disarm-and-submit. He'd have to strike Tai's weapon with his combat stick and dislodge it from her grasp. Such an aggressive strategy opened a combatant up, making him vulnerable to the same maneuver.

Zachary lowered his combat stick, inviting Tai to aim for his head. She took the bait and flicked the flexible baton up at Zachary's chin. In one quick motion, Zachary disengaged the friction locks on his boots and kicked off with his feet. Caught off guard, Tai wasn't fast enough to react, allowing Zachary to snare her weapon. With a thrust, he ripped the combat stick free from her fingers, leaving her prone and helpless. Zachary reactivated his friction locks and was in position to deliver the winning blow.

Buzz.

Time had run out. Zachary and Tai pushed off, down to the floor of the Qube, exiting through the antechamber into the holding room. All the Lightwing boys and girls, including Ryic, Kaylee, and the newly initiated Quee, were gathered there, along with their resident advisors.

"Congratulations, Tai," said Kwan, one of the boys' RAs. "You were in trouble there at the end, but the point total swung in your favor."

Tai's group of friends flocked excitedly to her side. Zachary wiped a bit of dried blood from his lip, feeling confident that he was still the better Starbounder. Tai hadn't taken out an entire fleet of Clipsian slicers, preventing Earth's destruction. But he had.

"Nice disarm," Kaylee said. "Now you've just got to

work on the submit part."

"Two more seconds and she would have been mine," Zachary said.

"You didn't hear me making excuses." Zachary didn't even have to turn to know that the voice belonged to Apollo, an obnoxious cabinmate of his who acted like they had some big rivalry going.

"That's because Tai kicked your butt so hard, Derek and Kwan had to help you out of the Qube," Kaylee replied.

"She did not," Apollo protested. "She blindsided me, is all."

"Who's making excuses now?" Zachary asked.

"Whatever. Second best is just a loser with bragging rights," Apollo said. He didn't give Zachary a chance to get in the last word, either; he was already halfway across the holding room.

"Tai Sunaka's mother was a Karteka warrior," Ryic said. "She fought off a whole army of snagglevire with nothing more than her knuckles and a bo. Tai was probably given her first combat stick when she was in diapers. It's a miracle you lasted as long as you did. I'd say second place is something to be plenty proud of."

"How did you take such a beating in there and keep fighting, anyway?" Quee asked Zachary.

"It comes naturally for me," he replied. "I'm a middle child."

∘ ∘ ∘

Later that day, during free hour before dinner, Zachary, Kaylee, Ryic, and Quee were practicing warp glove–wielding maneuvers on the pebbly beach between the boys' and girls' SQs. As had become customary for the foursome, they were hanging out by themselves, away from their fellow trainees.

"Is it just me, or have we gotten a little cliquey since we've come back?" Ryic asked. "We hardly socialize with anyone else here."

"That's because we have nothing in common with them," Zachary replied. "After all we've been through, what do we have to talk about? Who's going to be SQ captain, or what they're serving for dinner in the Ulam dining room tonight? It just doesn't seem that important."

Quee twisted her wrist and pointed at a row of soda cans resting on top of a rock pile in the distance.

"Remember, use your forefinger to adjust direction,"

Zachary said. "You don't need to aim with your whole hand."

In the weeks since Quee had been formally welcomed as an Indigo 8 Starbounder-in-training, she had received her very own glove, and only now was she starting to get the hang of it. Sort of. A black disc formed before her, and she reached her gloved hand through. But she overshot her target, opening a second hole about ten feet beyond the cans.

"Almost," Zachary said. "You just have to keep practicing. Here, watch. Notice how I don't rush my distance calibration."

He pulled a metal orb from his pocket and, with a squeeze of his pinky and thumb, the ball expanded, enveloping his hand in a tight-fitting green-and-silver warp glove. He pointed at the cans, then turned his wrist thirty degrees to set the distance. His glove opened up a pair of holes and darted through them. He grabbed one of the sodas, bringing it back to his side.

Kaylee walked up and snatched the can out of Zachary's glove. She used one of the sharp points on her spiked bracelet to punch a hole in the top.

"Thanks," she said, before taking a big swig.

Just then, Zachary's Indigo 8–issued tablet chimed. He pulled it out of his pocket and unlocked it with a swipe. He then touched a prompt that read INCOMING MESSAGE.

"Permission granted for off-base declassified communication," Cerebella said.

"She's talking about you calling your parents, right?" Quee asked.

"Indigo 8 takes its security very seriously," Zachary replied. "You can't just make a cell phone call anytime you please."

"You still planning on keeping your parents in the dark about Olari when you talk to them?" Kaylee asked.

"I don't have much choice," Zachary replied. "I know they'd tell Madsen, and you saw what happened the last time we trusted the IPDL. An assassin was sent to kill us. I still think there's a way my mom and dad can help us, though. And I won't even have to tell them the secret Olari was so desperate to protect."

"I don't understand," Ryic said. "Why do you feel it's necessary to deceive them?"

"Because if they suspect I'm in even the slightest bit of danger, they'll do whatever they can to protect me."

"Even if it jeopardizes the entire outerverse?" Ryic asked.

"Rational thinking gets thrown out the window," Zachary said.

Ryic's naivety made sense, considering he had no experience with how overprotective moms and dads could be when their kids were in trouble. Where Ryic came from, a distant planet called Klenarog, people didn't have parents. Instead, they were birthed from a primordial spring known as the Origin Pool.

"Well, if it makes you feel any better, Ryic, it doesn't make sense to me, either," Quee said, calibrating her warp glove for another attempt at grabbing a can. "The closest thing I had to parents in Tenretni was the gang of hustlers and thieves who took me in after I was abandoned. And they had me crawling through air ducts before I could walk."

"And I thought time-outs were bad," Kaylee quipped.

"I'm not complaining. They taught me how to survive. I never would have made it this far without them." This time when Quee reached her gloved hand for the can, she came up a few feet short, having miscalculated the distance again. But she was undeterred, lining up her glove once more.

"Do you regret leaving?" Zachary asked. "Coming here and starting over?"

"No. For the first time in my life I feel like I have a purpose. Like I'm doing something that matters. But I worry sometimes about forgetting where I came from, and who I was before."

"I think about the life I left behind, too," Ryic said. "I was going to be made supreme commander of my people. But I ran away, thinking this would be easier." He sighed. "That certainly hasn't turned out to be the case."

"We've all reinvented ourselves since we got here," Zachary said. "Well, everyone but Kaylee."

"That's not true," Kaylee said.

"Really?" Zachary asked. "Name one thing that's different about you."

"I tried this new shade of purple nail polish."

"Yeah, I don't think that counts," Zachary replied.

"I did it!" Quee shrieked.

The others turned to see her jumping up and down excitedly, holding one of the soda cans in her warp glove.

"What did I tell you?" Zachary said. "It's all in the wrist."

Quee smiled. She popped open the can and was met by a blast of carbonated fizz that sprayed her directly in the face.

○ ○ ○

Zachary was being led by a robotic attendant down an underground hallway in the Ulam.

"Beautiful day today, isn't it?" Zachary asked, making small talk. The robot continued its methodical walk forward without responding. "You don't get out much, do you?"

The two arrived at a small, enclosed room with a single seat before a holographic projector. "You just going to wait outside?" Zachary asked as he sat down in the chair. The robot inserted the double prongs sticking out from its fingers into the wall. "I'll take that as a no."

Within seconds, a face appeared on the screen. But it wasn't his mom or dad. It was his younger sister, Danielle, still a few years away from being old enough to attend

Indigo 8 herself. She was deaf, but that wasn't going to keep her from being a Starbounder. Nothing would.

What's up? Danielle signed.

Hey, sis, how you been? Zachary replied.

The same. Except I've been using the training room in the garage a lot more since you left. I even talked Mom and Dad into letting me put a mattress in there.

"And a minifridge," Zachary's mom added, appearing next to Danielle in the frame, along with Zachary's dad.

That hardly came as a surprise to Zachary. He could picture his old neighborhood now: all the kids riding their bikes outside, while Danielle blasted holes through a combot with her sonic crossbow.

"So, what do you need?" Zachary's dad asked, cutting to the chase. "I know you're not just checking in to say hi."

"I resent that," Zachary replied. "But now that you mention it, I could use a little extra cash in my canteen account. I totally shredded my last pair of friction boots."

"Uh-huh," Zachary's dad said. "I had a feeling."

"It's still great to see you, though," Zachary said.

"Not so fast, young man," Zachary's mom said. "You're going to have to tell us something about what you've been up to at Indigo 8 before we just send money."

"Well, I've really gotten into engineering. In fact, do you guys still keep in touch with that contact you had at the Inertia Starcraft plant on Adranus?"

"Arg-Nik-Vo," his dad responded. "Yeah, why?"

"The Lightwings are scheduled to go on a field trip to the Musuem of Quantum Engineering," Zachary said. "I'm sure it will be interesting and all, but I thought maybe you could pull a few strings with Arg-Nik-Vo and get us a guided tour of the real deal."

"You must *really* want those friction boots," Zachary's mom said. "Buttering up your father like that."

"Don't discourage him, dear," Zachary's dad said. "It sounds like he's taking a genuine interest. Of course I'll talk to him. He'd be thrilled to show a bunch of young Starbounders where all their cool gear comes from."

Please don't say "cool," Dad, Danielle signed. *It makes you seem anything but.*

"That's assuming Director Madsen will even sign off on the additional stop," Zachary's mom said.

"I can't see how that would be a problem," Zachary's dad replied. "It's great to see that you're so keen on engineering and astrophysics. Those were my favorite subjects, too."

Zachary just smiled and nodded. Little did his dad know, this trip would have nothing to with science.

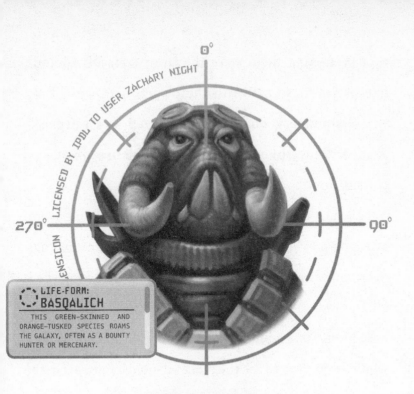

LIFE-FORM:
BASQALICH

THIS GREEN-SKINNED AND
ORANGE-TUSKED SPECIES ROAMS
THE GALAXY, OFTEN AS A BOUNTY
HUNTER OR MERCENARY.

«TWO»

"**W**hatever you do, do not, and I repeat, *do not* stray from the shadow path," the engineer known as Arg-Nik-Vo warned the thirty Lightwing boys and girls following behind him.

Zachary and his fellow Starbounders-in-training were walking under the sun-resistant cover of a breeze-way connecting their ship's docking station to the Inertia Starcraft manufacturing plant. Just beyond the reflective roof protecting them were the three suns of Adranus. Except for those native to the planet, like Arg-Nik-Vo, whose shimmery, quartzlike skin acted as a safeguard, exposure to the intense light would result in spontaneous combustion.

Zachary's plan had gone exactly as he'd hoped, and after the previously scheduled stop at the quantum engineering museum, here they were visiting the place where all the *real* IPDL fighter ships—pitchforks, battle-axes, dreadnoughts, and more—were built. Normally, Zachary would be excited to see the most talented engineers in the outerverse at work. But today, he had a more urgent matter to tend to.

"There it is," Quee whispered, pointing to a shimmering domed structure far beyond the boundaries of the shadow path. "The Exo-Shell factory where my hacking hands were manufactured."

"We'll have to sneak away once we're inside," Zachary whispered.

"Everybody, through here," Arg-Nik-Vo said. "And if you haven't already, make sure to remove your lensicons. We're entering a level-one clearance zone."

He held open a door leading from the breezeway onto the factory floor of the Inertia Starcraft plant. Zachary stepped inside and was awed by what he saw. Hundreds of ships in various states of construction filled the room, and giant sunbeams shone through the skylights, directed down at the metal exteriors of the spacecraft. Engineers of all species were spread throughout the facility. Those native to Adranus were able to work without protective gear, while the rest were covered head-to-toe in mirrored mesh bodysuits that reflected the heat away.

"Now you can see why the IPDL decided to build their ships here," Arg-Nik-Vo said. "The light from the planet's three suns heats the metal to a malleable state. It allows engineers to bend and ply the outer hulls to the exact shape they wish."

"I want *that* for my sixteenth birthday," Kaylee said, eyeing an ultra-sleek ship that resembled the open mouth of a cobra.

"Get in line," Arg-Nik-Vo said. "Those are strictors. They're chase ships, for Elite Corps officers only. They've outrun every spacecraft in the outerverse, even lunaracers."

"What's behind there?" asked Apollo. He was pointing to an area enshrouded by digital curtains.

"Your guess is as good as mine," Arg-Nik-Vo answered. "It's classified, even from high-level engineers like me. We've got a pretty extensive R and D pipeline. The projects are on a strictly need-to-know basis. And none of us need to know."

Zachary had turned his attention away from the ships on the floor. He was focused on finding an exit they could slip through unnoticed.

"Now we're going to move into the instrumentation wing," Arg-Nik-Vo said. "There you'll see how starboxes and Kepler cartographs are programmed."

He led the Lightwings toward a set of double doors on the opposite end of the floor. Zachary, lingering at the back of the group, was still searching for a way out when he felt a hand on his shoulder. He looked up to see one of the engineers, hidden behind the visor and helmet of a bodysuit.

"Did I do something wrong?" Zachary asked.

"Yeah," a voice replied. The engineer pulled Zachary behind a crate. Then the tinted visor slid open, revealing Kaylee inside. "You haven't suited up fast enough." She tugged Quee and Ryic back toward the same hiding spot. Both of them looked as surprised as Zachary did.

"Where did you get that?" Zachary asked.

"I used my warp glove to swipe it off the far wall by the decontamination showers. I suggest you do the same."

She pointed across the hangar to where there were a number of suits on hooks. Zachary, Ryic, and Quee activated their warp gloves as inconspicuously as they could and aimed, turning their wrists forty-five degrees. A black disc appeared before each of the young Starbounders and corresponding ones materialized near the bodysuits. Zachary reached his glove through the pair of holes he'd formed and retrieved an outfit. He swiftly put his on and felt a rush of cool air blow from an internal temperature regulator. Ryic had done the same thing. Quee, however, was still struggling with the trajectory of her warp glove, so Zachary used his own glove to grab one of the suits for her. Now the four were indistinguishable from the hundreds of workers filling the floor.

The last of the Lightwings followed Arg-Nik-Vo into the neighboring room, none the wiser to the missing trainees.

"There's an exit back there, by the strictors," Zachary said.

The four of them walked across the floor without attracting so much as a second glance. They never hesitated, heading straight out the door onto another shadow path, one that stretched about thirty yards before coming to an end.

The city laid out before them was a metropolis of sandstone buildings, constructed to withstand the intense midday heat of Adranus's three suns. There were no roads, only covered pedestrian walkways.

"Where are all the vehicles?" Kaylee asked.

"Too hot for them," Ryic replied. "They'd melt like butter. You saw what the suns did to that metal inside."

The group stepped out from the shadow path and into the sunlight. Zachary immediately felt the cooling jets inside his bodysuit pump faster to counteract the swelter. He and his friends headed for one of the other covered walkways, but before they reached it, Zachary watched as an untucked hoodie string, sticking out from the crack between Ryic's helmet and bodysuit, ignited. Like the fuse on a stick of dynamite, the string was incinerated, the flames moving swiftly toward Ryic's helmet.

With no time to speak, Zachary tackled his friend to the ground and squeezed the burning nylon in his fist, extinguishing it. Ryic looked stunned and confused until Zachary showed him the charred remains of his pull string.

"Everybody needs to be extra careful," Zachary said. "This isn't going to work if one of us comes back looking like a grilled cheese sandwich."

Zachary and Ryic got back to their feet and the four continued ahead. They took a covered walkway through a maze of buildings, passing Adranusians standing in line before vendors who were cooking slabs of unrecognizable food on the pavement just beyond the edge of the shadow paths. Even through his helmet, Zachary could smell the smoky aroma wafting up from the ground.

The walkway led to a roundabout that moved counterclockwise and could be exited from any of a dozen offshoots. Zachary and his cohorts stepped onto the rotating platform. Looking up, Zachary tried to judge which path would take them on the most direct route to the shimmering dome.

"Turn up ahead," Zachary said.

"No, wait," Quee interjected. "According to the maps we downloaded, there's a shortcut through the Hydration Bazaar."

Quee departed the roundabout at the next offshoot. The others were right behind her as they moved into a covered marketplace where liquids of every color were dispensed from freezer tanks into prefrosted mugs. Customers had to drink the fluids quickly before they evaporated in the near-boiling conditions. The group hurried through the crowded bazaar, arriving at the other side.

Quee was right. The shortcut through the bazaar had dumped them directly in front of the dome. A sign out front read EXO-SHELL.

"This is it," Zachary said. "This is the place."

The door slid open easily and the four walked into a dimly lit space. Once they noticed that all the skylights were closed, Zachary, Ryic, Kaylee, and Quee removed their helmets. Carapaces, robotic exoskeletons used to house alien life-forms, stood on display. Some were designed to look like real human bodies, while others were three stories tall, mechs apparently used for industrial lifting or combat. Several were open, showcasing the operational maintenance systems inside.

Zachary glanced around for an employee, but the only other life-forms appeared to be browsing customers. Until one of the carapaces began to move.

An eight-legged mech the size of a small car stomped forward. It nearly trampled Zachary, stopping only a foot in front of him. The exposed bronze gears covering its outside clanked noisily and the shield covering the pod at the center of the mech retracted. An Adranusian looked out.

"Apologies," she said. "Still working out the kinks in the latest model."

"We're looking for some information," Zachary said, "about some symbols on a pair of hands taken from a carapace."

Quee unzipped her bodysuit and pulled the robotic hacking hands out from a pouch slung across her chest. The Adranusian pressed a button within the mech and its legs folded in on themselves, bringing her to ground level. She climbed out and approached Quee.

"Let me see those."

Quee passed them over, and the Adranusian held them in her mirrored fingers. She took a long look at the grid of black-and-white squares on the knuckles.

"These hands come from a mech model we discontinued after too many of its drivers died in the battle of Siarnaq. The symbols are encrypted instructions that can only be read with lexispecs."

"Lexispecs?" Zachary asked.

"A precursor to the lensicons you wear today," the Adranusian answered. "Goggles with grid-pattern recognition technology. They're hard to come by now. They could only identify things that had already been coded for them. Not much use for them anymore."

"Do you know where I can find a pair?" Zachary asked.

"There's an antique collector a few blocks from here. In the underground at Cyan Circle. He'd be your best bet."

The Adranusian returned the hacking hands to Quee, and the four Starbounders-in-training put their protective helmets back on. This time Ryic made sure to tuck in his remaining hoodie string.

"Thanks," Zachary said.

The group exited and made the short walk to a staircase leading down to the Cyan Circle metro stop. Upon reaching the underground platform, Zachary removed his helmet again, trying to get a better look at the row of kiosks and small shops set up along one wall. One in particular caught his attention: a cluttered storefront with knickknacks filling the window. This had to be the antique shop. He started toward it.

Just then, a burlap bag was pulled over his head.

Zachary began to kick and thrash, swinging at his unseen attacker. His arms were gripped tightly and pulled behind his back. He felt the circulation drain from his wrists as they were bound with cable tie.

"Get off me!" Zachary heard Kaylee cry. Her voice was muffled, and from the ensuing sounds of struggle, he guessed that she, Ryic, and Quee had all been hooded and bound, too.

A blow to the back of Zachary's knees dropped him to the ground. His chest slammed into the tile floor of the underground as the muzzle of a weapon was pressed into his spine. Zachary's assailant moved in close to his ear. Through the mesh of the bag, he could feel the warm, rancid breath of his captor, who whispered, "Who else have you told?"

"I don't know anything!"

"That's not the question I asked," the baritone voice wheezed back. "The symbols on your arm. Who have you told?"

"No one!"

Zachary heard the unmistakable hum of a sonic crossbow being charged.

He only had a second to brace himself for the end. A blast was fired. But somehow, miraculously, Zachary was still alive.

Three more shots followed in rapid succession. A moment later, the bag was ripped off Zachary's head.

Arg-Nik-Vo was standing over him with a sonic crossbow faintly glowing in his hand. He used a razor-sharp blade on his forearm to cut through the cable tie binding Zachary's wrists. "Come with me now." Something told Zachary that Arg-Nik-Vo was more than just your average engineer.

As he stood up, Zachary looked over to see the creature that had attacked him lying lifeless on the metro platform. He was suited up, but his helmet's visor had slid open, revealing a flat-faced humanoid with green skin and orange tusks.

By the time Zachary had brushed himself off and processed how close he'd come to dying, Arg-Nik-Vo had freed Ryic, Kaylee, and Quee. Three other bodies littered the ground.

"Basqalich bounty hunters." Arg-Nik-Vo turned to Zachary. "Your parents asked me to keep an extra close eye on you, and I guess now I see why. Mind telling me what you were doing down here?"

"Would you believe it if I told you we took a wrong turn?"

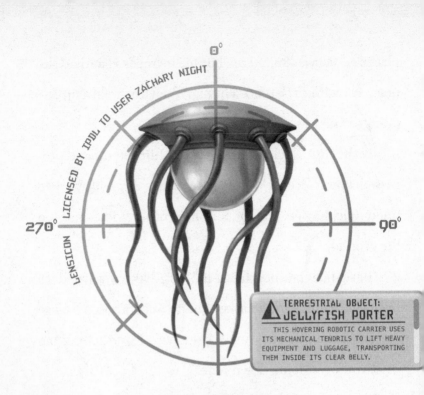

0°

270°

90°

⚠ TERRESTRIAL OBJECT:
JELLYFISH PORTER
THIS HOVERING ROBOTIC CARRIER USES
ITS MECHANICAL TENDRILS TO LIFT HEAVY
EQUIPMENT AND LUGGAGE, TRANSPORTING
THEM INSIDE ITS CLEAR BELLY.

«THREE»

The Skyterium was its usual hub of activity in the hour before lights-out. Starbounders from every SQ were scattered about, some looking up at the images displayed on the enormous telescopic lens that acted as the building's rooftop, others snacking and socializing, less interested in the astronomical phenomena above them.

Zachary, Kaylee, Ryic, and Quee were part of the latter

group, noshing on buttered popcorn and soft pretzels as they huddled in a corner booth around their Indigo 8–issued tablets. Kaylee's pet vreek, Sputnik, slurped unpopped kernels out of the palm of her hand.

It had been less than twenty-four hours since the Lightwings had returned from their field trip to Adranus. Arg-Nik-Vo never said anything about Zachary and his friends' little escapade, even when an Indigo 8 chaperone had asked point-blank where they'd been. And Zachary stuck to his story that they had been separated from the group and gotten lost. They never had a chance to check out the antique shop, either, but given the possibility that the Exo-Shell employee had set them up, the odds were good that the store never had lexispecs to begin with.

"Professor Olari wanted me to be able to decipher the message on my arm," Zachary said now. "He must have known that the only way to do that was with a pair of lexi-specs. Maybe he left one behind."

"His office has been packed up and put into storage," Quee said. "If he had a pair, that's where we'd find them."

"Aren't the storage units on a restricted level of the Ulam?" Ryic asked. The others all nodded, as if this was no big deal. "Please tell me you're not thinking about breaking into Olari's unit."

Quee inputted several touch commands on the surface of her tablet and suddenly all four of their handheld computers were synched to display the Ulam's floor plan.

"Have I ever mentioned how glad I am you're on our side?" Zachary asked.

"This'll be easy if we go after lights-out," Kaylee said after examining the floor plan. "RA patrol ends at midnight. Then it's just the aux-bots."

"And they won't be a problem," Quee said. "They're just machines. They'll be putty in my hands. But the locks on the storage units aren't computerized. They're reinforced padlocks."

"Then we'll have to get in the old-fashioned way," Kaylee said.

"What's that?" Ryic asked.

"Ion frost cannon," Kaylee replied.

"Just how the bank robbers from the 1930s did it," Zachary said drily. Ryic gave him a blank stare.

Zachary spied Director Madsen approaching.

"Behind you," Zachary muttered, clearing his throat.

Quee tapped the display on her tablet and all four screens switched from the incriminating maps to their weekly itinerary. Even Sputnik tried to look casual.

"Good evening, Lightwings," Madsen said. "You all look rather serious tonight. Up to anything I should know about?"

"No, sir," Kaylee replied. "Just reviewing our schedules."

"Mm-hmm." Madsen seemed less than convinced. "The four of you have become quite inseparable since your little adventure a few weeks ago. And now I hear you broke off from the field trip yesterday?"

"Saving the outerverse *is* a pretty serious bonding experience," Zachary said.

"Well, don't cut yourself off from the rest of your SQs," Madsen said. "You might have experienced something they haven't, but that doesn't mean they don't have plenty to offer."

Zachary wasn't so sure about that.

Madsen continued on, moving over to a trio of Darkspeeders who were playing a friendly game of hover dice.

"Attention, all Starbounders," Cerebella's voice called

over the PA system. "The Indigo Starbounder Games SQ captains have been chosen. You will lead your fellow Earth-based trainees against all the other Starbounder camps in the outerverse for a chance to claim the price-less Indigo Diamond trophy."

The far wall of the Skyterium lit up with a list of names. Everyone stopped what they were doing and hurried over to look—everyone but Zachary and his friends, that is. There was a whole lot of chatter, and then Apollo was marching past their booth.

"I've made my first official decision as Lightwing boys' captain," he said, smirking like a proud peacock. "I know who the towel boy is going to be."

He gave Zachary a playful punch in the arm that was clearly meant to leave a bruise then strutted off. Zachary stepped out from behind the table and pulled his retracted warp glove out of his pocket, activating it. The green-and-silver metal instantly extended down to his elbow and he reached his hand through a hole in space, pushing Apollo to the floor.

"Then I guess you won't mind me wiping the floor with your face."

Apparently Apollo was better at dishing out insults than taking them. He charged at Zachary with his head lowered, tackling him. The two tussled, trading blows. Other Starbounders formed a circle around them, the show on the ground far more entertaining than the one playing across the glass roof.

Ryic and a red-haired Lightwing named Chuck ran over and pulled Zachary and Apollo apart. As they cooled off, the mob of Starbounders dispersed, disappointed.

"He's not worth getting freighter duty over," Ryic said to Zachary.

"You need your Silly Putty buddy to protect you?" Apollo taunted. "This isn't finished." He pushed Chuck off and stormed away.

"Maybe we can petition for a recall," Quee said.

"We've got bigger things to worry about," Zachary replied, stroking the spot on his arm where the branded symbols were hidden beneath his sleeve. "Twelve thirty tonight. We meet at the equipment shed."

◦ ◦ ◦

Zachary lay awake in his hyperbolic sleeping pod, eyeing the translucent digital wall clock. He'd been counting down the minutes since lights-out. Just a few more and it would be time. Only two Lightwing boys had attempted to sneak out of the sleeping quarters since the beginning of the year. Kiev Petrovich made it only a few steps before he got busted by the RA on patrol. Rodney Hirsch had fared slightly better, steering clear of Cerebella's walkways and sticking strictly to the woods. The sole reason he got caught was that the Lightwing girl he was rendezvousing with had been followed by an aux-bot.

The clock flicked to 12:25 a.m. and Zachary gave a soft whistle to signal Ryic. The two tiptoed down from their upper bunks and moved quietly across the gray padded floor. Kwan and Derek were asleep in the RA pods closest to the SQ's six-sided door. Just as the door automatically opened, a voice whispered from behind.

"Where are you going?" It was Chuck, sitting up in his bed, groggy and half-asleep.

"You're dreaming," Zachary whispered. "We're not even having this conversation."

"Whatever you say." Chuck's head hit the pillow and he was snoring within seconds.

Zachary and Ryic continued on, careful to avoid

Cerebella's black glass sidewalk. They hunched low and hurried across the manicured lawns into the woods. The two stumbled through the trees, moving as fast as they could.

"Zachary, it's too dark," Ryic whispered. "I can't see a thing."

"We're almost there."

But Zachary had spoken too soon. Just as they came out of the cluster of trees, they found themselves face-to-face with an aux-bot. Zachary froze, but Ryic wasn't fast enough. He tripped right into its line of sight. This was it. Just like Kiev and Rodney before them, they'd be another cautionary tale to dissuade Starbounders from sneaking out.

Then the aux-bot did something unexpected: it turned and kept going.

"Quee!" Zachary exclaimed under his breath. "What would we do without her?"

It was only a short distance to the equipment shed, where Zachary could already see Kaylee and Quee waiting in the shadows. Zachary and Ryic hustled over to meet them.

"We've got ten minutes before those aux-bots reboot," Quee said.

The four ran over to the front door of the shed and found it unlocked. Kaylee turned the handle and they entered carefully. The inside looked more like a high-tech armory than a place used to store water skis. One wall had a row of photon bows hanging on a rack; another had belts with stun balls affixed to them. And a pair of ion frost cannons—metal hoses attached to handheld, ice-encrusted tanks—rested on the floor.

Kaylee slipped one of the tanks over her shoulder like a backpack, taking the hose in her hand. Zachary grabbed a belt loaded down with stun balls. Ryic looked at him curiously.

"Just in case," Zachary said.

Quee picked up an aux-bot repair kit, and the group exited as quietly as they'd entered. They traveled under the cover of the woods as far as it would take them before they were forced to make a break across a wide-open field. The Ulam was nearly within reach. They crossed the parking lot, ducked around the reflecting pool with the figure-eight fountain, and hustled up the steps leading to the building's main doors.

Zachary pulled open the door and the group headed into the Ulam's large foyer. The satellite projections of the other Indigo bases that were typically displayed on the wall had been turned off for the night. The only illumination came from the stars shining through the clear glass ceiling and the footlights glowing beneath the Outerverse Memorial of Lost Planets, a series of planet sculptures inscribed with the date and circumstance of each planet's destruction.

Zachary, Kaylee, Ryic, and Quee walked briskly onto the open platform waiting on the ground floor. Zachary said, "B-thirty-seven," and the platform immediately began descending.

Zachary watched as the basement levels of the Ulam passed them by. Quick flashes revealed familiar destinations, like the flight simulation training arena, and places Zachary had never visited, like the subterranean gardens that grew all of Indigo 8's fruits and vegetables. Hundreds of feet later, the platform came to a stop.

The group exited onto one of the many restricted floors. It was nondescript, with cold steel walls and long xenon tubes flickering on the ceiling. Dozens of pad-locked doors lined the hall, each one labeled with either a name or a general description of the contents held within. Zachary and his companions scanned the labels until they found the one with EXCELSIUS OLARI written on it.

"I'd stand back if I were you," Kaylee warned the others.

They stepped away, giving Kaylee room to charge her ion frost cannon. She aimed the tip of the nozzle at the door and gave the regulator a squeeze. A hissing blast of subzero air shot out, encasing the steel lock in a win-tery cloud. Kaylee reharnessed the hose and Quee came forward, pulling a vibration hammer out of the aux-bot repair kit. She lifted it and took a forceful swing at the chilled padlock. Upon contact, the crystalized steel shat-tered, falling to the ground in countless pieces.

Zachary gave a push and the door opened inward, revealing Olari's darkened storage unit.

"Activate infrared on your lensicons," Zachary said.

"We have that?" Ryic asked, surprised. "So that's how everyone else in the SQ gets to the bathroom without a night-light."

Zachary blinked in sequence and his view instantly changed. Suddenly the storage unit was bathed in a bright-green glow. It was only then that they realized it was empty.

"Where's all his stuff?" Ryic asked.

"I don't know," Zachary replied. "Maybe we're in the wrong unit."

"No, this is definitely it," Kaylee said. "We're just too late. Somebody must have gotten here first."

Zachary searched the room for anything that might have been left behind as a clue. Finally he noticed a dusty imprint on the outside of the door. He leaned in for a closer look. Even with his infrared, he was just barely able to make out three letters: B.A.S.

"I found something," Zachary said. "It looks like whoever pushed open this door before us had some sort of initials embossed on their sleeve. B.A.S."

"I can cross-reference the Indigo 8 roster and see if there's a match," Quee said.

"Our ten minutes are almost up," Ryic said. "We should really get back to our SQs."

Zachary scanned the room one last time, even though

he knew he wouldn't find anything else. Their only lead was a set of all-too-common initials.

Kaylee had already returned to the hallway to sweep up the padlock shards with her hand. She deposited them in the aux-bot tool kit, so that the only evidence of their break-in was the missing lock on the door.

The group hurried back to the landing at B-37, where the open platform waited. They got on board and Zachary stated, "Main level," sending the inclinator rising rapidly.

"Who would be interested in Professor Olari's stuff besides someone who knew about his secrets?" Kaylee asked.

"I don't know, but whoever it was had the key for that storage unit," Zachary said.

The platform came to a halt at the foyer level of the Ulam and the four young Starbounders got off, rushing for the exit. Before they reached the doors, a soft buzzing sounded from Quee's wristwatch.

"Those aux-bots are going to be back on patrol," she said.

They raced out the door on high alert, sprinting across the open field toward the woods leading to the equipment shed. Their plan was to dump the ion frost cannon and the rest of the tools they'd borrowed, then split up and take separate routes back to their SQs.

Zachary leaped over roots and fallen branches. He heard a thud behind him and turned to see that Quee had taken a tumble. Kaylee was already by her side, helping her up and pulling her along. But the sudden burst of noise had drawn the attention of a nearby aux-bot, which was searching with the spotlight on its forehead and zipping through the trees.

There would be no way to outrun it, especially for Quee, who was now limping on a bad ankle. So Zachary reached down to the belt he had swiped from the shed and pulled off one of the stun balls. The aux-bot was coming at them with frightening speed. Zachary whipped the ball at its metal exterior and the electrically charged projectile made contact, frying the aux-bot's circuits with a hiss and a flash of light.

"We're going to be under siege within minutes," Quee said. "They send signals to one another every thirty seconds. As soon as the rest of the patrol realizes one of the bots is down, they'll come to its last known location."

But Zachary had no intention of waiting. He took off running again and the others followed behind him. Kaylee helped pull Quee along, and soon they reached the equipment shed, tossing the "borrowed" goods inside without even stopping to make sure they were back in the right place.

"Be careful," Kaylee said to the boys.

She gave Zachary's hand a quick squeeze, then ran off with Quee's arm around her shoulder.

Zachary stood, watching them go for as long as he dared. His hand was tingling. There was something different about the way she had touched him.

"Come on," Ryic urged.

Zachary took off in a sprint, but it felt like he was flying.

∘ ∘ ∘

Zachary and Ryic stood at one of the breakfast serving stations in the dining hall. Zachary was piling eggs and bacon on his plate, still feeling the high from the previous night's covert mission. There was something especially gratifying about outsmarting Cerebella and doing it alongside his best friends. Ryic stayed in line only to keep him company, content with the heaping portion of what looked like regurgitated spinach already filling his bowl.

"They're late," Ryic said, eyeing the door. "I'm starting to worry."

"Kaylee probably just overslept," Zachary replied.

"What if they got caught? Madsen could be interrogating them right now." Ryic was getting more nervous by the second. "They'll come for us next. I won't be able to lie. I'll cave like a Sentropian mine."

"Morning," Kaylee said, coming up behind Ryic.

He jumped. "You're here."

"Sorry," Quee said. "Accessing all of Indigo 8's personnel files took longer than we expected. Cerebella initiated some new data scramblers. Don't know if it has to do with what we did last night, but finding one of their aux-bot's circuits stir-fried probably raised a few red flags."

"So, what did you find?" Zachary asked.

"Only one match," Quee replied. "A Cometeer girl named Becky Alice Samuels."

Quee pointed one of her three bony, reptilian fingers toward an older blond girl sitting with some friends across the hall.

"We could talk to her," Zachary said. "See what she knows."

"What if B.A.S. are the initials not of a person," Ryic asked, "but of a place or a thing?"

Zachary and Kaylee looked at him impatiently.

"*Someone* had to leave that mark on the door," Zachary said.

"Exactly," Ryic said. "But it's much more likely that a uniform's sleeve would have the initials of an organization on it than the initials of a person."

Quee was already typing furiously on her tablet.

"I can set up an algorithm to see if anything in the outerverse database has those initials." She continued tapping away. "On second thought, I'll limit the results to the Indigo Sector so we're not waiting literally forever." She waited as the tablet processed the search. "Three hits. The Ba'al Asteroid System. The Bendavid Archer Space Station. And . . ." Quee paused.

"What is it?" Zachary asked.

"The Black Atom Society," she replied.

Immediately, Zachary remembered the questions he had been asked upon his return to Indigo 8 after his close call on Callisto. One of the inquisitors in particular, a mysterious masked figure, wanted to know if Zachary had any connection to the Black Atom Society, a shadow organization of scientists.

Kaylee and Ryic had been grilled about the very same thing.

"Their last known base of operations was in one of the six unnamed galaxies beyond the Tundra planets, on a moon called Luwidix." Quee looked up from her tablet. "According to Indigo 8's most recent manifest, a dreadnought made a delivery there just a few days after Olari's death. It was signed for by someone named Bedekken."

"Then Luwidix is where we need to go," Zachary said. "Any more ships scheduled to make the trip?"

"Not officially," Quee replied.

"We just need to get to a space station," Zachary said. "It doesn't matter which one. Once we've bounded into the outerverse, we can always find a skipjack to get us the rest of the way."

"But our next field trip isn't for weeks," Ryic said.

"We're not waiting for our next field trip," Zachary said.

°°°

It was free hour before lights-out, when all of Indigo 8's Starbounders-in-training typically met up in the Skyterium. But Zachary, Kaylee, Ryic, and Quee were down on the field just outside the Ulam.

Zachary felt his bones shake as a mechanical tendril struck the side of the luggage porter he had commandeered. Ryic, who was sitting beside him in the glass belly of the hovering, jellyfishlike robot, nearly got jolted into his lap. Kaylee and Quee were controlling the porter that had smacked them; the two giant makeshift mechs were engaged in a no-holds-barred grudge match, giving new meaning to breaking the rules.

"Tendril number seven, strike," Zachary directed the porter.

His vehicle responded on command, lashing out and hitting the transparent bubble below where Kaylee and Quee were seated.

The first trainees were beginning to leave the Skyterium and gather on the steps of the Ulam, watching the highly reckless exhibition unfolding before them. And they were loving every minute of it, cheering on each subsequent blow. Soon the crowd had grown so big that it spilled over into the parking lot.

A tendril from Kaylee's porter grabbed ahold of Zachary's ride and gave it a tug, spinning it like a top. A dizzy Ryic clutched his stomach, but Zachary was smiling. He had spotted a line of furious RAs and Indigo administrators rushing outside to put an end to their defiant display.

"What do you think you're doing?" shouted Mr. DiSalvo, Director Madsen's right-hand man. "Get out of there right now."

Kaylee got in one last swing, then both porters shut down, slowly lowering to the ground. The four young Starbounders climbed out and were swiftly met by DiSalvo, whose dark eyebrows furrowed angrily.

"Come with me," he said.

DiSalvo led them back toward the Ulam, pushing through the throngs of onlookers. But before the group reached the steps, Madsen was already approaching them.

"This behavior is totally unacceptable," he said, angrily. "Ever since the four of you returned from your mission, you've been acting like a bunch of arrogant hotshots. And

I'll tell you right now, that is *not* what being a Starbounder is all about."

"We were just having some fun," Zachary said.

"Well, I hope it was worth it," Madsen replied. "You just got yourselves freighter duty."

Zachary made an effort to look extra disappointed. He didn't want Madsen to know that this was exactly the punishment he wanted.

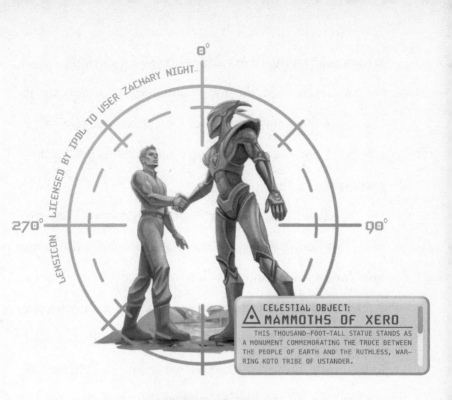

0°

270°   90°

△ CELESTIAL OBJECT:
MAMMOTHS OF XERO
THIS THOUSAND-FOOT-TALL STATUE STANDS AS
A MONUMENT COMMEMORATING THE TRUCE BETWEEN
THE PEOPLE OF EARTH AND THE RUTHLESS, WAR-
RING KOTO TRIBE OF USTANDER.

«FOUR»

Zachary, Kaylee, Ryic, and Quee followed DiSalvo through Indigo 8's enormous underground space hangar, which was even busier than usual with takeoffs and landings. Accompanied by flight instructors, older trainees were taking pitchforks out for practice runs. While his fellow Lightwings would be spending the morning between their warp glove–wielding class and the starchery range, Zachary and his friends would be mopping up lunar mold off the floors and ceilings of a starjunk.

As DiSalvo led the four young Starbounders up to the vessel, Zachary got a closer look at the massive barge, equipped with retractable solar sails and large shipping containers.

"You'll be reporting to Captain Aggoman," DiSalvo said. "And don't worry, we made sure to check the cargo hold for any alien fugitives this time."

DiSalvo pointed them toward a ladder leading up to a porthole. They ascended the rungs and climbed aboard. Once inside, they were greeted by a tough-looking woman with scars covering her face and what looked like a square speaker surgically implanted into her windpipe.

"They tell me you've already done this once before," her synthesized voice said. "Well, just so you know, I'd prefer it if you didn't crash this ship. I'm Captain Aggoman."

She extended her hand and greeted each of them in turn.

"Mag mops are in the hold," Aggoman continued. "There'll be plenty of time to swab the decks after our first bound. Why don't you head down there and strap in?"

"What happened to your throat?" Quee asked bluntly.

Zachary winced, but Aggoman didn't seem offended. In fact, just the opposite.

"Molking raiders," she said. "Three geigernades hit before I even knew we were being attacked. The shrapnel turned my face into Swiss cheese. And put a hole through my larynx. I'm lucky to be alive."

Zachary started for the steps leading down to the hold. The others followed.

"By the way," Aggoman said, "I heard about your little stunt with those porters. You're either the stupidest Starbounders I've ever met . . . or you've been bitten by the zero-G bug and you'll find any excuse to go three folds deep in space. So, which is it?"

"I guess we're just dumb," Zachary said.

Aggoman looked at him through narrowed eyes, sizing him up. "Somehow, I doubt that."

Zachary, Kaylee, Ryic, and Quee departed the atrium just beyond the porthole and moved deeper into the bowels of the starjunk. The ship was populated with about two dozen crew members, the majority of whom were busy strapping down an enormous sphere inside the cavernous interior cargo hold.

"What's that?" Ryic asked a passing deckhand.

"A shield generator," the man replied. "We're delivering it to Indigo 5. Since Nibiru's attack on Earth, the IPDL has decided to beef up security on all the Indigo training camps and bases."

It made sense. If the Callisto Space Station hadn't been protecting Indigo 8, it was very likely that Zachary's home planet would have been annihilated. He had never thought about how vulnerable some of the outerverse's smaller bases must be. He was glad to see that the IPDL wanted to take every precaution, defending each of their allies with the most advanced technologies coming out of Indigo 8's engineering level. That's why the Starbounders existed, after all—to protect those in the outerverse who could not protect themselves.

Aggoman's voice echoed over the starjunk's loudspeaker.

"We've set our course for the day. We'll be making two bounds to the Xero system, where we'll stop to refuel. Then it's two more to Indigo 5. The first fold should be opening momentarily, so please harness in for takeoff."

Crew members finished tightening the straps holding

the shield generator in place before moving over to individual seats built into the walls. They pulled down overhead harnesses that looked like the kind on amusement park roller coasters. Zachary, Kaylee, Ryic, and Quee found their own spots along the wall and locked themselves in. Unlike the previous ships they had traveled on, there were no windows in this hold for the crew to look out of. Beyond the rumbling Zachary felt as the starjunk's motors initiated their ignition sequence, the only way he could confirm that they'd started moving was through the live-feed monitors attached to the armrests of each chair.

Zachary watched as the freighter accelerated down one of the space hangar's launch tubes. A crew member sitting nearby, his arms thick and his head shaved, looked over at the trainees.

"Hey, I know you," he said. "You're those four kids." He turned to his shipmates. "Check it out. Look who we got here."

A few of the other deckhands glanced over and nodded with looks of recognition. Zachary held his shoulders a little higher. Perhaps he didn't get recognition at Indigo 8 for saving Earth, but at least his reputation preceded him in the outerverse.

"You're the ones who got that entire dreadnought crew killed," the intimidating crew member continued. "I promise you this—something goes down here, I'm getting off this ship alive before any of you do."

Zachary shrugged. "Gee, what more do you have to do to get some respect around these parts?" he asked.

The rest of the crew had already dismissed them, returning their attention to their view-screens.

On the armchair monitor, Zachary could see an enormous black disc form, just like the ones created by their warp gloves only a thousand times bigger. This was the galactic fold that would send them hurtling into space. With a burst of speed, the starjunk bounded through.

○ ○ ○

Over the past few weeks, Zachary had been getting as comfortable in zero gravity as he was on Earth. Each time he returned to space, it felt like he was home. It didn't matter if it was a galactic field trip or mop duty on a starjunk; he was just happy to be in a place where friction boots were the only things holding him down.

Zachary, Kaylee, Ryic, and Quee were on the lower

deck, mopping the floors, walls, and ceilings. It was the first time they had been alone since getting on the ship.

"IPDL freight charter rules mandate that every registered crew member be given a twenty-minute leave during fueling stops," Quee said. "That should give us plenty of time to sneak away and figure out how we're going to get to Luwidix."

"Once Aggoman reports back to Indigo 8 that we've gone AWOL, I'm guessing they'll send IPDL officers to find us," Zachary said, sliding his mag mop along the wall, cleaning up a large glob of green slime and depositing it into a bucket. "We'll have to make a few bounds to lose them and hope we can disable the tracking beacon on whatever ship we steal before they catch up."

"Are you sure about this, Zachary?" Ryic asked. "Why are we putting ourselves in so much danger for a mission that randomly fell into our laps? What if Olari didn't even have a pair of lexispecs?"

"Clearly the Black Atom Society thought there was *something* in Olari's possessions worth stealing," Zachary said.

"But why does it have to be us?" Ryic asked.

"'Cause we're Starbounders," Zachary replied.

"This is still about the good of the galaxy, right?" Kaylee asked.

"What's that supposed to mean?" Zachary snapped back.

"I just want to be sure all this saving the outerverse stuff isn't going to your head."

"You don't have to worry about me. My feet are planted firmly on the ground." Zachary glanced up and realized he was, in fact, standing on the ceiling. "Well, not literally. But you get the point."

Kaylee was about to reply when she stepped into a viscous pool of jelly sticking to the wall. The goo made a squishing sound and covered her boots.

"This is disgusting," she said.

Ryic swiped a finger across his shirtsleeve, where a drop of the substance had drifted. Then he licked it clean off. "Mm, asbesmoss," he said.

Neon-blue lights started to blink throughout the ship.

"You know what that means," Kaylee said. "It's bounding time."

"I really wish I hadn't just eaten that," Ryic said.

While Ryic occasionally regurgitated his second stomach during jumps through interdimensional folds, Zachary actually found the wholly unnatural sensation exhilarating. The four returned to the main hold, where they took their seats once more alongside the starjunk's crew members as the ship made the leap through space. After the usual disorientation of a bound, Zachary acclimated himself, watching the starjunk exit into the rosy-hued cosmos of the Xero system on his armchair monitor.

The blue lights stopped blinking, indicating that it was okay to move freely about the cabin once more.

"You four," one of the ship's engineers called from a nearby doorway. "Float your butts over here. I need hands to release the fueling valve. We'll be docking within minutes."

The trainees soared across the cabin, ducking beneath a metallic archway and passing through a series of soundlocks, doorways that muted the loud commotion of the ship's propulsion generator. As they moved from one antechamber to the next, the noise grew louder until they reached the near-deafening engine bay, where a large silver object resembling a tuba reverberated from what sounded like bombs exploding inside of it. As Zachary had learned in his Indigo 8 quantum physics class, this was a miniature particle accelerator, much like Earth's Large Hadron Collider, which shoots electrons at near light speed. Aux-bots were tending to the outside of it, under the engineer's supervision.

"I need each of you to twist one of these valves open manually!" the engineer shouted over the blasts.

"Isn't that what you have the aux-bots for?" Zachary asked.

"Darn right it is," the engineer replied. "But you four are here on disciplinary duty. Which means you're no better than these dumb hunks of metal."

Zachary got to work on the first one, but even with the wrench he was handed, it was a struggle. His cohorts didn't seem to be faring any better. The engineer turned to Ryic with a worried look on his face.

"Hey, Stretch, wrong valve!" he yelled. "What are you trying to do, flood the whole engine bay? Stick to the square-shaped caps, not the round ones."

Ryic corrected himself, and the four trainees finished

the task at hand, but not before callusing their fingers and blistering their palms.

"The bots will take it from here," the engineer said.

Zachary, Kaylee, Ryic, and Quee returned to the top deck and found other crew members gathering there. Even Aggoman had pulled herself away from the flight command to join them. And Zachary was beginning to see why.

As the starjunk made its approach toward the floating IPDL hub, a truly remarkable sight came into view. An enormous statue, perhaps a thousand feet tall, formed an arch above the docking bay. It depicted two colossuses shaking hands: one human, the other some kind of alien species.

"The Mammoths of Xero," Aggoman explained, seeing the look of wonder on Zachary's face. "A monument to the truce agreed upon when the people of Earth encountered the Koto tribe of Ustandar, formerly known as the Wild Planet. Up until then, the Koto had been a ruthless, warring species. It was the first formerly hostile group that mankind recruited into the IPDL. As a tribute to friendship, this statue was erected—a gateway of peace for all those who enter."

The ship was moving in closer and the full scope of the monument, in all its intricate detail, was becoming clear. It was as if Michelangelo himself had carved the meteoric rock one section at a time. All around the hub, aux-bots were jetting through the sky on flying motorcycles, only stopping to do maintenance on the docked spacecraft.

"I think my dad told me about this place once," Zachary interjected. "He said that one of my ancestors was part of the crew that brokered the peace."

"Maybe that's him," Ryic said, staring at the human half of the towering statue. "It certainly looks like you."

Zachary hadn't seen the resemblance before, but now that Ryic mentioned it, there were some uncanny similarities. He and the statue had the same chin, the same cheekbones—even its eyes mirrored his own.

"Actually, that's Io Mech," Aggoman said. "Nobody could ever confirm where he came from, but he's considered by many to be the greatest Starbounder who ever lived."

The starjunk made its final descent, coasting beneath the torsos and arms of the monument. It slowed its approach and pulled into a waiting airlock. Once the ship came to a complete stop, the crew members began to file for the exit. Zachary, Kaylee, Ryic, and Quee started to follow them, but Aggoman signaled for them to stop.

"Fueling stop leave is only mandatory for crew members," she said. "And the four of you are just here on disciplinary duty."

"So we're stuck?" Kaylee asked.

"You've got work to do," Aggoman replied. "Let's see if you can't get the flight deck and navigation room spotless while they're unoccupied."

The four trudged back to where they'd left their mag mops. As soon as they were out of earshot, they conferred.

"Now what?" Ryic asked.

"We'll have to duck out the cargo hold," Zachary said.

"It's not going to take Aggoman long to realize we're not here," Ryic replied.

"That's why we have to move fast," Zachary said.

They scooped up their minimal belongings and floated toward the cargo hold of the ship. Several crew members were already hauling bricks of fuel inside with the assistance of robotic carriers only slightly larger than

Indigo 8's hovering jellyfish porters. Other deckhands were pushing empty fuel containers off the ship. The trainees stopped just out of sight.

"There's no way we walk out that door without being seen," Quee said.

"Who said we're going to walk?" Zachary replied.

He got down low and pulled himself behind the first obstacle he could find, leading the others to one of the empty fuel containers waiting to be taken off the ship. Zachary lifted the top of the container and confirmed that it was large enough to hold all four of them. He climbed inside first, then lent a hand to Quee. Ryic and Kaylee vaulted themselves in next.

Once they were all hidden inside, Ryic stretched out his arms and pulled the top back on, securing it as best he could. The walls and floors of the bin were still slick with gasoline. Zachary had manned the pump at the corner station for his mom and dad plenty of times before, and the smell reminded him strangely of home. But the nostril-burning odor was also making his brain hurt.

The four waited silently. Zachary could hear tendrils latching onto the outside of the container, then a voice.

"Let's take 'em out," it said.

And then they were moving. Neither Zachary nor any of his companions said a word. They merely braced themselves as the fuel bin left the ship and gravity suddenly returned, sending Quee, Ryic, and Zachary tumbling on top of Kaylee. She had to bite her tongue to keep from squealing.

"What was that?" a second voice outside asked.

The container was set down abruptly. Zachary peered through the tiny grating and saw a pair of crew members approaching. He flashed two fingers to Kaylee, who lifted up her pant leg and revealed a vibration hammer that she'd conveniently forgotten to return to the aux-bot repair kit. She pulled her retracted warp glove from her pocket and let it slide over her arm. Then, in one fluid motion, she formed a hole and stuck the hand clutching the vibration hammer through. She struck the closer of the two crew members in the back of the neck, knocking him unconscious. The other guy immediately sprinted for a distress panel on the far wall, but before he made it there, Kaylee had created a new hole behind his head and dropped him to the ground as well.

After the second thud, Ryic pushed off the top of the container and the four young Starbounders peeked out to survey their surroundings. They had been transported to the IPDL hub's refinery, where dozens of identical bins were stored. For the moment, they appeared to be alone.

Zachary, Kaylee, Ryic, and Quee climbed down to the ground. Together they lifted the fallen crew members and deposited them into the empty crate. Once the lid was back in place, they pushed the container across the floor so that it blended in with all the others.

"They're going to be okay, right?" Ryic asked.

"Nothing a little Tylenol won't cure," Kaylee replied.

Quee was scrolling through her wrist tablet. "This is bad. This is very bad."

"Could you narrow that down to something more specific please?" Zachary asked.

"I'm looking at the hub's manifest. That starjunk we just flew in on is the only ship docked here," she said.

"I don't understand," Zachary said. "I saw tons of other ships surrounding the hub on our approach."

"Yeah, but none of those are actually docked. They're just free-floaters. You'd need a space ferry to get to them."

"We can't wait around for another spacecraft to arrive," Ryic said. "So what do we do?"

"Quee, any idea where we can find some bio regulators on this hub?" Kaylee asked.

"Why?" Ryic asked nervously. "You're not suggesting we make an untethered space jump, are you?"

"I'm not that crazy," Kaylee replied. "I was thinking we'd get a ride." She pointed through the refinery's window to a pair of aux-bots zipping through space atop their flying motorcycles.

"Oh, that makes me feel *much* better," Ryic said.

"Looks like they've got bio regulators at every emergency exit," Quee said, scanning her tablet with a few deft flicks of her fingers.

"What about the bikes?" Zachary asked.

"The aux-bot service portal is below the hub's customs terminal," Quee replied. "There's a stairwell next to the confiscated goods room that should take us directly inside."

"Lead the way," Zachary said.

With one eye on her tablet and the other reading the signs at every turn, Quee guided them past unsuspecting hub workers toward the nearest emergency exit. Zachary spied a glass case affixed to the wall housing a half dozen bio regulators, clear mouthpieces that formed repulsive barriers around any creature, human or otherwise, who placed the device in its mouth. They were essential for survival in the vacuum of space. Each of the four Starbounders took one before Quee was on the move again.

They hustled across the hub's central platform, where most of the station's visitors and temporary residents were watching some kind of broadcast breaking on the holographic displays.

"Protos, a colonized planet and member of the IPDL, was thrown into darkness after its sun was suddenly and inexplicably drained to a third of its size," an outerverse reporter said from behind a news desk.

Zachary paused briefly to take in the news, but he didn't have time to listen for more. As he continued to walk, Zachary took note of the structure's labyrinth of transparent tubular walkways that crisscrossed above and below them. Every path had a clear view of the Mammoths of Xero through the domed rooftop.

Zachary caught sight of Aggoman passing through a tube about two stories above. He suddenly realized there was nowhere to hide.

"Just keep your head down and walk," Kaylee said, following Zachary's gaze and coming to the same conclusion he had.

Fortunately, everyone around them was still distracted by the broadcast.

"The answers to what caused the stellar disaster remain unknown, but the Intergalactic Science Federation is sending a team there now, along with IPDL relief forces," the outerverse reporter said.

Zachary again paid little attention to the story as he passed; all that mattered to him was that it was keeping all eyes away from him and his fellow Starbounders.

Quee led them to a junction point where a glass tube descended from the platform and spiraled downward to the customs terminal. The four followed it as quickly as they could. When they arrived at the customs gate, a humanoid agent clearly not from Earth was performing cranial identification scans on all those who passed. An orange light meant the individual had clearance to enter.

A blue light meant the opposite.

"Let's turn around," Zachary said. "There has to be another way."

"This is no problem," Quee said confidently, punching the keypad of her wrist tablet. "Just follow my lead."

She stepped up to the agent who was holding the electronic scanner. The agent waved it across Quee's forehead and Zachary was surprised to see it glow orange. Zachary wasn't sure how, but Quee had somehow tricked the system. He just hoped that whatever she had done would work for him, Ryic, and Kaylee, as well.

Zachary was next, and he stood before the agent as coolly as he could. The electronic device moved from one edge of his hairline across his forehead to the other. He could hear the faint hum of the scanner working, then watched as the light miraculously turned orange once more.

Ryic and Kaylee were cleared the same way, allowing the four to enter the customs terminal. They headed a safe distance away from the checkpoint.

"How did you do that?" Zachary asked Quee in a whisper.

"I discovered a long time ago that if I ever wanted to step foot anywhere besides bottom-tier Tenretni, I'd have to figure out a way to make myself invisible. So I implanted a recombinant chip right below my temple to scramble DNA scanners." Zachary hadn't given it a second look before, but now he couldn't take his eyes off the thin scar above the bridge of Quee's nose. "Before I walked through, I just turned up the frequency a little, so the device synched with my recombinant chip and lost the ability to discern those with clearance from those without."

The customs terminal was a spacious room filled with boxes, bags, and crates. Officials used ostrils, long-nosed, batlike creatures, to sniff out any contraband hidden within. If the goods were deemed permissible, they got pushed across the terminal for their owners to retrieve them. Those declared illegal were sent to the confiscation room. Which was exactly where Quee was leading Zachary, Kaylee, and Ryic. But that wasn't the destination she had in mind. It was the doorway just beyond it.

The four slipped into the stairwell, and just as they did, an official called out, "You're not supposed to go in there!"

The door closed behind them and they broke into a sprint down the steps. They reached the entrance to the aux-bot service portal, and each of the young Starbounders inserted their bio regulators into their mouths. Just then, the hub's emergency alarm started to wail, no doubt alerting the station's security forces to their escape.

Zachary put his warp glove–encased hand into the indentation beside the door, causing it to slide open. He was fully aware that he'd be leaving a digital DNA trail for anyone who came looking for them, but there was no other way. He and his companions stepped through an atmospheric atrium, a small isolated room where gravity could be gradually adjusted to acclimate new visitors to the station. When they came out on the other side, the four were suddenly floating in a completely silent hangar where aux-bots were boarding and docking their flying motorcycles. The walls were lined with machinery and tools that the robots could use for any requested repairs to the hub and all its surrounding ships.

Zachary pushed off the wall and soared across the room to one of the unoccupied bikes, straddling it. He signaled the others, and they joined him with mixed success and not nearly as much style. Thankfully, these aux-bots seemed to be programmed only for maintenance, not security—not a single one gave the trainees a second glance.

Zachary, Kaylee, Ryic, and Quee pressed the ignition buttons on the sides of their handlebars and jetted out through the hangar's open bay doors. Zachary had always imagined that riding on a motorcycle would be a spine-tingling experience, feeling the rush of wind blowing through his hair and the ground vibrating beneath the bike's tires. But this was a thrill of a different kind. With no up or down, there was only forward.

Quee had taken the lead again, guiding them toward a small, free-floating jumpcraft. There were plenty of other ships, bigger and faster-looking, but this one resembled a model they'd recently used in a flight simulation class at Indigo 8. Zachary blinked twice.

⚠️ **CELESTIAL OBJECT: SKIPJACK**

THIS ALL-PURPOSE COMMERCIAL SPACECRAFT IS USED BY BOTH THE IPDL AND CIVILIANS ALIKE.

There would be no slowing them down. At least, that's what Zachary thought until a pulse vibrated through his motorcycle and shut down the engine. While it didn't affect his bike's speed, it did leave him unable to control its direction.

Zachary glanced over his shoulder and saw where the blast had come from. Three bucklers, small IPDL patrol ships with particle cannons and stun disruptors, were in pursuit. Quee, Ryic, and Kaylee, now aware of the danger behind them, began zigzagging to avoid the steady bursts shooting from the bucklers' disruptors. Zachary had no choice but to continue on a straight path, one taking him far afield of the skipjack, directly toward the side of an idling battle-axe. He tried to wave down his friends for assistance, but it appeared they were too preoccupied to help.

Zachary's flying motorcycle was fast approaching the battle-axe's sharpened blade. The impact would kill him for sure. The only solace was that it would be quick. But Zachary was going to make one last gamble. He balanced his friction boots on the bike's seat and steadied himself in a standing position. As Kaylee weaved her vehicle out of the way of another blast and into Zachary's proximity, he pushed himself off and just floated, desperate and dangling, for a terrifying few seconds. But his timing was perfect; he was scooped up on the back of her passing cycle.

Quee and Ryic were the first to reach the outside of the skipjack. They quickly dismounted their bikes and clung to the ship. By the time Kaylee had pulled up alongside them, Ryic and Quee had already unlocked the secured entrance portal and were slowly sliding open the door. The bucklers were still trying to immobilize the young Starbounders, but it was too late. The four had boarded the getaway vessel and resealed the portal behind them.

Once inside, they removed their bio regulators. Zachary and the others soared for the flight deck. They could hear the sound of the ship getting hit from the outside.

"Kaylee, activate the defense shields," Zachary said

as he buckled himself in. "Ryic, prepare the cloaking mechanism."

Zachary began sweeping his hands in front of the gesture recognition display. The skipjack stirred awake, lights blinking on, and suddenly the ship was moving. Once Kaylee had initiated the skipjack's defenses, she flipped on the Kepler cartograph, which showed all the nearby suns and galactic folds.

More fire was coming their way, but most of the damage was being deflected by the repulsive shields.

"What's taking you so long? We need that cloaking mechanism!" Zachary barked at Ryic.

"I'm looking. The control panel is set up differently from the flight simulation model."

Another trio of blasts ricocheted off the exterior of the ship, causing some of the displays to momentarily malfunction. When they stabilized, Kaylee was pointing to a pair of tubes on the Kepler cartograph.

"There are two adjacent holes up ahead," she said.

"I've got an idea," Zachary replied as he steered a course for the closer one.

"But those bucklers are still right behind us," Kaylee

said. "They're going to know exactly where we're going."

"That's what I'm counting on," Zachary said.

They were about halfway to the galactic fold when Ryic clapped his hands.

"Found it!" he exclaimed, jamming his fist against a button on the far wall.

A cool blue tint filled the ship. As soon as he was sure the skipjack had turned functionally invisible, Zachary shifted directions, taking them toward the second galactic fold. The three bucklers fell right into his trap, continuing straight for the first. Zachary had no idea where the pursuing ships were bounding for.

But one thing was certain. The Starbounders were no longer being followed.

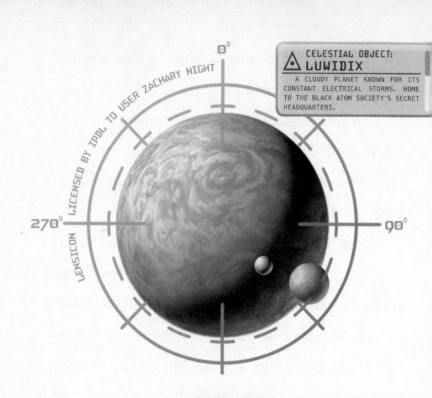

270°

0°

90°

«FIVE»

The skipjack had made three additional bounds since losing the IPDL hub's security, and now it was floating listlessly through the cosmos, undetected and unbothered.

"Luwidix is here," said Kaylee, indicating a glowing spot on the cartograph. "I've mapped the fastest route, which uses these four galactic folds. We should be there in an hour."

Zachary was eager to finally get to the Black Atom Society headquarters. Somewhere within that secret organization's walls were Olari's belongings, and with them, hopefully, the lexispecs needed to decipher the message on Zachary's arm. If the professor's warning was as dire as it sounded, then every minute that went by without answers was a minute closer to some unspeakable evil. But knowing that he and his companions were the only ones standing in the way of that threat didn't intimidate him. It exhilarated him.

"You're welcome, by the way," Kaylee said to Zachary.

"Oh, thanks," Zachary replied. Then he got a confused look on his face. "What am I thanking you for exactly?"

"I don't know. Just rescuing you from oblivion?"

"Right. That."

"If I hadn't flown by when I did, they would have been scraping you off the windshield of a star freighter," Kaylee said.

"Well, then consider us both lucky," Zachary said.

"I'm not sure I follow," she replied.

"I avoided becoming a space pancake. And you still have me around to school you in everything."

Kaylee scoffed. "Maybe I shouldn't have saved your butt."

"They are so mean to each other," Ryic whispered to Quee, loud enough for Zachary to hear.

"That's how human males and females let someone of the opposite sex know that they like them," Quee replied.

"What a strange way of showing it," Ryic said. "I don't think I'll ever understand their species."

"Who ever said anything about us liking each other?" Zachary asked, blushing.

Just then, a scruffy, bearded man entered the flight deck, pointing a static harpoon at them. "You got three seconds to explain yourselves."

Zachary and his companions were all caught off guard.

"We thought the ship was unoccupied," Quee finally managed.

"Why would that give you the right to take it?" the man asked.

"We're Starbounders," Zachary said. "We had to commandeer your ship for official IPDL business."

"If you think being associated with those autocratic rubes helps your cause, I've got a static harpoon that'll make you wish you'd given me a different answer."

The man took aim with his harpoon, which crackled with electricity, and started to pull back his arm.

"We'll pay," Ryic said.

It was enough to give the man pause. "What currency are you offering? Indigo chips or serendibite?"

"Whichever you prefer," Ryic replied. "Sir."

The man lowered the harpoon. "In that case, the name's Wayfare. I rent my ship by the hour."

The man hung his weapon on one of the ship's wall harnesses, and the four young Starbounders were able to relax.

"Seeing as how we're going to be sharing oxygen, mind telling us what you're doing with that shock rocket?" Kaylee said, eyeing the harpoon. "Weren't those banned after the Vert-Gemini Implosion?"

"Sounds like somebody studied up on the Helio Wars," Wayfare said. "I use it only for hunting. Terra whales, mostly. Heard rumors that there's still a great white one out there. I'm close. I'm going to find it soon."

"How long have you been looking?" Zachary asked.

"Don't know. I stopped counting after the seventh year."

The man threw his head back and laughed. Zachary and Kaylee exchanged a glance. Zachary was pretty sure they were thinking the same thing: Of all the free-floating ships outside the IPDL hub, why did they have to pick this one?

● ● ●

Zachary stared out the flight deck window, watching as the skipjack passed by a cluster of icy white planets that looked like snowballs hanging in space. These were the tundra planets, and although it was impossible to see anything on their surfaces from this great distance, Zachary had no trouble imagining the swarms of vreeks that must be teeming down there, scurrying across the frosty dunes.

"Once we make our final bound, we'll arrive in Luwidix's solar system," Kaylee said. "According to the galactic database, direct atmospheric landings are prohibited due to the intense electrical storms that ravage the planet daily. But there's a fold that connects directly to a hangar beneath the Black Atom Society. We may be able to slip through and land undetected, depending on how tight the security is."

They didn't have to wait long to find out. They only needed to get within a thousand miles of the space fold in question to see a ring of dangerous-looking particle turrets suspended around it.

"Even if this ship's cloaking mechanism was top-of-the-line, those gunners have distortion sensors," Wayfare said. "We'd never get past them."

"So I guess slipping through isn't an option," Quee replied.

The group turned to look out at the cloudy planet of Luwidix slowly rotating as it orbited around its distant yellow sun. Flashes of electricity crisscrossed the globe as balls of lightning arced through the swirling gray.

"Is it possible to calculate the odds of us getting struck on the way down?" Ryic asked.

A flurry of bolts zipped across the planet's atmosphere.

"I'm no mathematician, but I'd venture to guess one hundred percent," Wayfare said.

"Do you think the ship could survive being hit?" Kaylee asked.

"All the equipment would be fried," Wayfare replied. "It'd be like trying to fly a brick."

"But there's a chance we'd make it?" Kaylee asked.

"You're renting this ship, not wrecking it," Wayfare said.

"I have another idea," Zachary said. "Got any ejection suits in here?"

"There are two," Wayfare answered. "Why?"

"Because we won't have to worry about the equipment if we leave the ship here and free-fall."

"That's crazy," Ryic said, before Wayfare had a chance to. "You're going to parachute through an electrical storm?"

"If those suits follow standard IPDL safety guidelines, they'll have metal ribbing lining the exterior," Zachary said. "Any current would be conducted outside of our bodies, preventing damage to vital organs. Hypothetically."

"I'll go with you," Kaylee said.

"And I was just about to volunteer," Ryic added, none too convincingly.

"Not to acid rain on your parade," Quee started to say, "but—"

"Actually, the expression is just 'rain on your parade,'" Kaylee interrupted.

"Not in Tenretni," Quee said. Then she turned back to Zachary. "Let's say you do make it to the ground safely. How do you plan on getting back up?"

"Keep the ship outside of that space fold," Zachary said. "We'll find a way out."

"Am I the only one who thinks this plan is insane?" Ryic asked.

"No, it's insane," Quee replied.

"I stopped questioning whether Zachary's plans were sane a long time ago," Kaylee said. "Nothing could be crazier than blowing a hole in your own ship to get away from a fleet of slicers, and that turned out to save us all."

The skipjack sped closer to Luwidix. Wayfare had left the flight deck, only to return moments later with the pair of ejection suits, blue-and-silver rubber body gloves with thin metal strips going down the spines, arms, and legs. Zachary and Kaylee each took one and slipped it over their clothing. Then they placed protective glass helmets over their heads. The ship went into orbit safely above the storm raging below.

"We'll be waiting for you," Wayfare said. "But if you don't make it back within twenty-four hours, I'll assume you're dead and take these two to the nearest space station."

Zachary gulped. But if Kaylee was scared, she wasn't showing it. If anything, she looked like she was ready to go. The two soared down to the entrance portal of the ship. They stood before the glass divide that was the only thing between them and the thin atmosphere above Luwidix. Zachary hadn't realized it until now, but the ship had dipped low enough for them to start feeling the effects of the planet's gravity.

"So, you know how to open these chutes?" Kaylee asked through the helmet's headphone speaker.

"I was going to ask you the same thing," Zachary replied.

They shared a nervous laugh. Both did once-overs on the suits, and Zachary found a black button by the wrist with a picture of an open parachute on it.

"This must be it," he said. "And looks like there's an altimeter to let us know when to activate it. Once we touch down, with any luck we won't be far from the Black Atom Society. At least according to my warp glove's internal compass."

Wayfare's voice piped in over the ship's intercom. "We're in position. Time to fly."

Zachary and Kaylee waited for the entrance portal to slide open. As soon as it did, Zachary felt a whoosh of air. A single thought crossed his mind: how thankful he was that he wasn't afraid of heights, since the distance he'd be falling was impossible to gauge. But even more unsettling was the fear that he wouldn't make it halfway down without being vaporized, turned into nothing more than ash and dust. At least he'd be going down in a blaze of glory.

It seemed to Zachary as if he'd been standing there lost in his head for minutes, but it had been only a moment. Then Kaylee was jumping. Zachary snapped out of his daze and leaped into the void behind her.

At first, the sensation of rocketing through space was the ultimate adrenaline rush. But uncertainty set in once Zachary hit the clouds. He could no longer see Kaylee. In fact, he could hardly see an arm's length in front of him. Other than the gray, only the flashes of lightning were visible. The rush of wind whipping past his helmet was interrupted by the sound of thunderous booms. Zachary could feel his body falling faster. He glanced at his altimeter and the numbers scrolling rapidly across it. No signal yet. Then came a crash and a flash at the same time. Zachary had been hit. His entire body went rigid. The muscles in his legs trembled and his arms convulsed. His nostrils were filled with the scent of ionized oxygen and burned hair. Pain was running up and down his spine, but thanks to the metal conduction strips in his suit, he was alive.

Zachary was just beginning to recover when another bolt made contact. This one jostled his insides, making him feel like fainting and puking at the same time. The shock seemed to linger even after the numbness faded, and Zachary was starting to wonder how much more he could take. A third and fourth charge tested his resolve, sending a wave of searing heat from his toes to his shoulders, electrifying every nerve ending.

Finally Zachary came out of the clouds, and his altimeter began to beep almost immediately. His fingers were still twitching from the lightning, but he was able to will them to the black button by his wrist. He activated the chute release and suddenly a Kevlar kite shot out from the backpack attached to the jumpsuit. Zachary was tugged upward, then began to descend again at a much slower pace. As he drifted toward the ground, he spied Kaylee's parachute in a heap, with a single friction boot sticking out one of the sides. He steered himself in the direction of his friend. Kaylee didn't seem to be moving, just lying there, limp.

Zachary's toes were the first thing to touch down, but he skidded for close to a hundred yards before taking a tumble and rolling to a stop. He jumped back up to his feet as fast as he could, stripped off the backpack and helmet, and went running for her.

"Kaylee!" he shouted.

Once he reached her, he pulled the parachute aside and found her helmet-first in the dirt.

A sudden flood of guilt washed over him. This had been his idea, and she had backed him even when the others had raised their doubts.

He flipped her over, ripped off her helmet, and to his immediate relief saw that she was breathing.

"Kaylee, it's me," he said.

She blinked her eyes and stared up at him.

"Now I know what a surge protector must feel like," she said.

Zachary smiled and helped her into a sitting position.

"Just take it slow," he said. Nearby, another lightning bolt struck the earth. "Okay, maybe we should save the slow for later."

He hoisted Kaylee to her feet and disconnected her parachute. He checked the compass in his warp glove and verified the Black Atom Society's location. Then he looked up the slope ahead of them and saw a building with thousands of metal poles jutting out from its roof. Every few seconds, the storm sent bolts coursing through the different rods. There weren't any roads or pathways leading to the building, just a desolate landscape charred black from the relentless electrical assault. Zachary and Kaylee hurried for the hill, making themselves moving targets for the static blasts raining down from the sky.

"This is suicide," Kaylee said.

"No," Zachary replied. "The closer we get to that building, the *safer* we'll be. Those rods are there to draw lightning toward them. Which means *away* from us."

He was right. As the two neared the Black Atom Society, the sparks continued to hit the forest of metal towering above them. Zachary and Kaylee reached the front of the building, only to find a smooth wall with no door. They ran along the outer perimeter until they came across a hatch leading down into the ground. It might have seemed unusual that a site housing such advanced technology was unguarded, except for the fact that only the most daring or foolish trespassers would attempt what Zachary and Kaylee had just done.

Together, the two heaved open the hatch and descended a staircase into a hallway covered floor-to-ceiling in green rubber.

"We know someone named Bedekken signed for Olari's stuff," Zachary whispered. "So that's who we need to find."

"We'll save you the time," a voice called from behind them.

Zachary and Kaylee spun around to see two figures, one a charcoal-skinned Clipsian wearing a lab coat, the other a broad-shouldered, seven-foot-tall woman coming at them with a stun stick. Kaylee was hit first, and the nerve-numbing blow sent her into instant paralysis. Zachary reached into his pocket for his warp glove, but before he could defend himself, the stun stick struck his neck and he, too, went down. His face hit the rubber floor with a cushioned but firm thump.

What happened next felt like a nightmare made real. He was awake. He could see and hear everything happening around him. But he couldn't move. Not a single muscle. That meant he couldn't scream, even though he wanted to.

The giant woman hoisted Kaylee over one shoulder and Zachary over the other, then she and the Clipsian walked through the hall. It was hard to tell which direction they were headed, seeing as how Zachary's head was upside down and pressed against the woman's back. He could make out flashes of activity in the rooms they passed, mostly what looked like experiments being conducted. There was one exception that caught Zachary's attention: behind a thick glass window, a dozen robots tended to a family of cinderbeasts, ash-colored, bearlike creatures common throughout the outerverse. But unlike any cinderbeasts Zachary had seen before, these were emaciated, perhaps even dying. Zachary focused the crosshairs of his lensicon on a purple icon glowing on the window, and he used all his energy and concentration to blink twice.

Well, it made sense that the Black Atom Society had robots doing this research. They weren't technically life-forms, so no harm could come to them.

The woman carrying Zachary and Kaylee continued ahead, moving through a series of doorways before arriving at their destination: a lab room coated in black rubber. There were cages with lab rats and alien species inside. The woman set Zachary and Kaylee down on the floor.

It wasn't long before Zachary could feel a tingling in his toes, and soon sensation was returning to the rest of his body. He and Kaylee sat up almost at the same time. They shared a concerned look but didn't speak a word. The Clipsian and the large woman stood by silently. Then a third figure entered the room, but this one was no stranger. It was the same masked man who had questioned them at Indigo 8 all those weeks ago.

"We found these two in the tunnels," the Clipsian said to the masked man. "Somehow they made it to the planet's surface alive. They came in through the service hatch. We'll send out a search party to locate their ship."

The masked man walked up to Zachary and Kaylee. He stared down at them. Either he didn't remember them at all, or he was just doing a really good job of pretending.

"If you're lost, your memories will be erased. If you're trespassing, you'll be held here indefinitely. If you're spies, you'll be killed. So which is it?"

Zachary didn't like any of the options, so he remained quiet.

"Would the two of you please leave us alone?" the masked man asked the Clipsian and the woman.

They nodded and exited. Zachary and Kaylee had been left unrestrained. Either this was the height of arrogance and stupidity, or the masked man was even more dangerous than Zachary first suspected.

The masked man waited for the door to close. Then he leaned in close to the two young Starbounders.

"I'm sorry about my little display just then. But there are traitors within the Black Atom Society. I don't know who I can trust anymore." Zachary knew the feeling. "I'm guessing your visit here has something to do with our mutual friend, Excelsius Olari."

"Are you Bedekken?" Zachary asked.

"I am."

"We know that you received a delivery of Professor Olari's belongings," Zachary said. "He had a pair of lexi-specs. We need them."

"What for?" Bedekken asked.

"And why should we trust you?" Kaylee shot back.

"You shouldn't. But I assure you, we want the same thing. I know Excelsius had been working on something before his death. I offered my assistance, but he was incredibly paranoid near the end. Turns out he had every right to be."

Zachary and Kaylee shared a look. What choice did they have?

"He branded a message into my arm," Zachary said. "His lexispecs are the only thing that can decipher it."

"Then I'll bring them to you at once," Bedekken said. "You need to stay in here, though. Keep up the appearance of being under my custody."

Zachary and Kaylee agreed. Bedekken wasted no time. He was out the door. Zachary could hear his voice just outside.

"I'll be right back. Our visitors have decided not to cooperate. Perhaps I can persuade them to be more forthcoming with my tools."

"Or you could just give me a few minutes alone with them," Zachary heard the giant woman reply.

"No. I'll handle this."

Bedekken's footsteps faded into the distance, and Zachary and Kaylee were left alone.

"It's hard to trust a man wearing a mask," Kaylee said. "Even if you can see his eyes through it."

"Those creepy leather gloves don't help," Zachary replied.

The two waited. As the minutes crept by, Zachary began to wonder if Bedekken was ever going to come back with Olari's lexispecs. Maybe they had been played. Maybe Zachary had fallen right into Bedekken's trap, telling him what they had come for, and now he was off making sure they would never find it. Zachary scanned the room for another avenue of escape, but it appeared they were as trapped as the test subjects scratching at their cages across the room. The only way out was through the door guarded by the seven-foot-tall woman. Zachary and Kaylee could take her. Or at least try. Perhaps the element of surprise would give them the upper hand.

Zachary was palming his retracted warp glove, considering his next move, when the door opened and Bedekken returned carrying a small briefcase. He walked over to Zachary and Kaylee and set it down.

"My tools," he said. Bedekken popped open the case, revealing a pair of lexispecs. It looked like a pair of glasses without the arms and with three layers of fine crystal lenses, each with circuits running across its surface. "I think this is what you've been looking for."

Zachary removed the lexispecs and brought them up to his eyes. Tiny clamps locked onto his brows and cheekbones, holding the device in place. Zachary rolled up his sleeve and tilted his arm so he had a clear view of the grid of black-and-white squares. A scroll of holographic text appeared. But it wasn't a simple message. It was a dense nest of blueprints and mathematical formulas. What little he could understand didn't add up to much.

"It looks like plans for something that was being built," Zachary told the others in a hushed tone. "But it may as well be written in Chinese. It doesn't make any sense."

"Perhaps you would allow me," Bedekken said.

Zachary removed the specs from his eyes and handed them over. Bedekken lifted his fingers to the edge of his mask and pulled back the iron shell covering his face. He was human, but scarred and burned beyond recognition.

"An unfortunate hazard of working on Luwidix," Bedekken said. "I should never have stepped outside."

He clamped the lexispecs to his eyes and peered down at Zachary's tattoo. He took in the data that had puzzled Zachary just a moment ago.

"You're right," Bedekken said. "These are blueprints. Olari must have secretly retrieved them. I had no idea this was happening here, right under my nose."

"What?" Kaylee asked.

"It seems someone may have been building a kinetic force sink," Bedekken replied. "With the right power source, such a device would be capable of pulling all the heat from an entire city."

Zachary's mind was racing. Professor Olari must

have known that something with cataclysmic potential was being constructed inside the Black Atom Society. Obviously he didn't know who was building it, exactly. That was the task Zachary and his companions had been left to figure out.

"What if the sink had unlimited power?" Zachary asked. "Could it extinguish a whole sun?"

Bedekken looked up from Zachary's arm. "You've heard about the disaster on Protos?"

"Do you think it could be related?" Zachary asked.

"Perhaps. Whoever did that would have needed something extraordinary," Bedekken answered.

"Like a perpetual energy generator?" Zachary asked.

A look of grave concern crossed Bedekken's face.

"Yes, that would do the trick," he replied.

"Skold," Zachary said under his breath.

In his heart, Zachary had always had a feeling they'd be hearing about the alien fugitive again. He had saved their lives at the Callisto Space Station, but he had stolen its perpetual energy generator, too. It was one of the few of its kind, and no doubt worth a fortune on the black market.

"You think he could have been involved in what happened on Protos?" Kaylee asked.

"Skold is a profiteer, not a killer," Zachary replied. "But he might be able to lead us to whoever *was* behind it."

"I think you're right. You find who has the perpetual energy generator, you'll find who's responsible for Protos's sun going out," Bedekken said.

0°

270°

90°

◌⊃ LIFE·FORM:
GREEBOK
THE OUTERVERSE'S MOST COMMON
SPACE CATTLE, THIS LARGE-HOOFED
AND -HORNED BEAST IS ALSO USED
IN BLACK-MARKET BAREBACK-RIDING
COMPETITIONS.

«SIX»

Even though they were just for show, the shockles now clamped around Zachary's wrists were emitting frequent bursts of energy, making his fingers twitch uncontrollably. Kaylee's hands were immobilized as well, and she looked even less pleased with the painful restraints. Bedekken exited the lab room with his two prisoners in tow. The tall woman and the Clipsian remained stationed at the door.

"Where are you taking them?" the woman asked.

"I'm going to expedite their transfer to an extraction center," Bedekken replied. "Make sure there's nothing these two are hiding."

"Do you require our assistance?" the Clipsian asked.

"No, I can take it from here." Bedekken pressed a small button on a handheld device, causing the shockles on Zachary's and Kaylee's wrists to fire off a sudden charge. Both flinched. Once Bedekken led them down the hall and out of the others' sight, he leaned in quietly. "Sorry about that."

Bedekken hurried them through three more corridors, passing scientists of different species, each too busy to give them a second look. Zachary couldn't help but glance their way, though, his curiosity piqued by the shrouded gurneys they were pushing in and out of lab rooms. A bony tail reached out from beneath the plastic sheeting on one of the gurneys and poked at Zachary's leg. He hustled closer to Bedekken.

"What was that?" Zachary asked.

"I'm not sure," Bedekken answered. "There are so many experiments being conducted, it's impossible to keep track of them all."

"If the Intergalactic Humane Board knew what was going on here, they'd shut this place down so fast," Kaylee said.

"They do know," Bedekken said. "And they agreed unanimously to allow us to continue our work unmonitored. The research we're doing is for the good of the outerverse. And while the thought of it might not be pleasant, it's necessary."

He pushed them through a set of double doors and down yet another hallway. Up ahead was the entrance to a small space hangar.

"I'll procure us a ship and get us out of here," Bedekken continued. "We should be able to make it three bounds away before they realize we're not headed for an extraction center."

"Our friends are waiting for us in a skipjack just beyond the nearest space fold," Zachary said.

"Then we'll signal them to follow us," Bedekken said. "We won't have time for a rendezvous."

Bedekken stopped before a glass barrier at the end of the hall and jutted his masked face forward, allowing the optical scan to read his iris. Immediately the glass partition descended into the floor.

He ushered Zachary and Kaylee into the hangar, which appeared to be functioning as both a launch portal and a high-tech mechanic shop. One side had your standard-issue noncombat starships; the other, dreadnoughts, pitchforks, and various crafts Zachary had never seen before, all with their weapons and engines disassembled. A variety of workers, both organic and mechanical, were busy building prototypes with the old parts and new ones composed of pulsing glass and glowing metal.

Bedekken gestured across the hangar to a launch-ready starship that resembled the cylindrical head of a sledgehammer. "We'll be taking that one over there, the sledge. Just keep your eyes down and follow me."

They started toward it but were quickly stopped by a fair-skinned, red-haired woman who appeared to be carrying an invisible object in her arms.

"What's this?" the woman asked, eyeing Zachary and Kaylee.

"Trespassers," Bedekken replied. "I'm taking them to Gation 6. What are you doing back so soon?"

"We had some bugs with the new transparency silk. It becomes visible under high-level gamma radiation. Back to the drawing board."

They shared a smile and went their separate ways. Bedekken continued his approach toward the sledge when the red-haired woman called out from behind.

"I'm sorry, but I have to ask. If those are trespassers, why are only their wrists shockled? Protocol code two-forty-four clearly states that any prisoners must be secured at both the wrists and the ankles."

Bedekken stopped, then whispered to Zachary and Kaylee. "Get on that ship and don't turn back. I'll deal with her. Find whoever took that perpetual energy generator. Finish what Olari started. I fear this is bigger than any of us imagined. Go!"

Zachary and Kaylee didn't wait another moment. They were sprinting for the sledge. Behind them, the red-haired woman had pulled her sonic crossbow, but Bedekken was tackling her to the ground.

It wasn't until Zachary reached for the spacecraft's door handle that he realized his wrists were still shockled. Of course, Kaylee's were, too. But Bedekken was in the midst of a brawl that was keeping him a bit preoccupied at the moment.

Despite his limited range, Zachary was able to jimmy the door open, and he and Kaylee hurried on board. The two entered the flight deck and Zachary examined the steering mechanism.

"With our hands shockled, neither one of us will be able to fly the ship on our own," he said.

"Then we'll have to do it together," Kaylee replied.

Kaylee sat down in the pilot seat but made sure to take up only half of it. Zachary settled in beside her, and although it was a tight squeeze, it would have to do. They strapped the single seat belt across both of their waists, and their shoulders were pressed up snugly against one another.

With Zachary adjusting direction and Kaylee handling altitude, the pair gestured with their hands and motioned for takeoff. At first, the sledge lunged erratically, as their coordinated commands weren't quite synchronized.

"Slow down," Zachary said.

"How about you speed up?" Kaylee countered. "We're trying to get out of here alive."

They gave it another go. This time Zachary watched Kaylee's hands and she watched his. Outside, several of the hangar mechanics had apprehended Bedekken, and a few others were trying to signal Zachary and Kaylee to stop. The young Starbounders ignored them and together navigated the sledge toward the galactic fold. Zachary peered out the corner of the flight deck window to catch a final glimpse of Bedekken. Whether or not he suffered the same fate as Olari, Zachary would remember him as a hero, and make sure others did, too.

Zachary let his hands drift forward, increasing the ship's speed toward the fold. Suddenly the flight deck's lang-link hummed to life and a voice called out, "Surrender now. You are making an unauthorized exit. Return to Luwidix immediately."

Paying the warning no heed, Zachary and Kaylee hurtled the craft in the direction of the black disc hovering at the end of the tunnel and shot through once they arrived. Their bound took them into space, and as soon as the nose of the sledge exited the fold, the ring of particle turrets began an all-out assault.

"Inverted roll, z-axis," Kaylee commanded.

"What?" Zachary asked.

"I can't do it without you."

Zachary racked his memory. He knew he had learned this maneuver in his Indigo 8 flight class. As he was sitting there, momentarily frozen, the sledge got hit by another burst of fire, sending them spiraling rapidly. Once they stabilized, Zachary suddenly recalled every detail of making an inverted roll. But it was a little too late for that now.

More particle fire was coming their way. Only this time he didn't need Kaylee's prodding.

"Solar dive, sixty degrees," Zachary said.

Kaylee nodded and the two crossed their arms, allowing the ship to corkscrew downward, out of the range of the turrets. Safely in the clear, Zachary and Kaylee were able to breathe easier. For the first time since they'd shared the pilot seat, Zachary realized just how closely he and Kaylee were pressed up against each another. He tried to scoot aside to put a little distance between them, but seeing as they were buckled together, he didn't have far to go.

"I sure am glad I wore deodorant this morning," Zachary said.

Kaylee smiled, a bit uncomfortably.

Zachary's cheeks began to flush, but his embarrassment didn't last long. Up ahead, he could see Wayfare's skipjack. Zachary activated the flight deck's lang-link and sent out a message to the ship.

"Wayfare, it's us. We made it."

After a short silence, Wayfare's voice responded: "Well, I'll be a son of a gun. I thought you'd be goners for sure."

"Follow us to the next fold," Zachary said. "Quee and Ryic can join us then."

"Roger that," Wayfare replied.

Kaylee was already projecting the Kepler cartograph on the flight deck window, studying the colored tubes connecting distant points. "Let's head through here," she said, pointing to the nearest fold.

Kaylee and Zachary steered the sledge toward it, with Wayfare following behind. As they glided forward, Zachary spied an open underbin with various tools scattered inside, including a pair of magnetic tweezers that, with some clever maneuvering, could free them from the shockles. Zachary was about to call Kaylee's attention to it when she shifted her weight, grazing her arm along his. He felt his heartbeat quicken and decided not to say anything. Now that they were out of harm's way, what was a few more minutes?

° ° °

The stolen sledge and Wayfare's skipjack were floating beside each other in a dark spot of the outerverse. An O_2 bridge connected the entrance portals of the two ships, and Ryic and Quee were heading across.

"Good luck finding that terra whale," Ryic called back to Wayfare.

"You ever spot one, my lang-link's always on," he replied.

Ryic and Quee completed the zero-G transfer safely to the other side and the bridge retracted back into the sledge. Zachary and Kaylee, hands now free from the shockles, welcomed their friends with hugs.

"So, what did you find out?" Quee asked.

"Someone within the Black Atom Society was building a kinetic force sink," Zachary said. "Kind of like a vacuum cleaner, but instead of sucking up dirt, it sucks in power. Now, say it was attached to something like the perpetual energy generator that used to power the Callisto Space Station, which is like a big, big, big battery. Well, it would be capable of draining all the heat from a sun."

"Is that what destroyed Protos?" Ryic asked.

"We don't know for sure, but it's certainly what we're banking on," Zachary said.

"And we think Skold might be able to lead us to whoever's responsible," Kaylee added.

"Skold?" Ryic asked.

"There's a good chance the perpetual energy generator he stole from Callisto is in the hands of somebody very dangerous," Zachary said. "We need to locate that device before any more damage is done."

"There's been an IPDL manhunt for him since he escaped Callisto," Ryic said. "If they can't find him, how will we?"

"I thought we'd start back at the Fringg Galaxy Void Market," Zachary replied. "See if that black market trader—the one who hooked him up with the fuel—can help. Maybe she's heard from him."

The four Starbounders had returned to the flight deck, where Zachary retook the pilot seat and Kaylee began mapping the fastest route to the Fringg Galaxy.

They buckled in for the several-hour flight, and between bounds took shifts eating and sleeping. Well rested and fed, they arrived at their destination. Although it was unmarked on the Kepler cartograph, Zachary remembered just where to steer the sledge, toward the extra black patch of space with no stars. It was the camouflaged exterior of the void market. Zachary navigated the ship closer, right up until he could discern the black outline of the enormous space structure.

Zachary waved his hand in front of the lang-link and requested permission to enter. All he and his friends heard in response was a series of beeps and whirring sounds.

"I know that language," Quee said. "It's hacker codex." She leaned toward the flight deck control panel and replied with her own series of whistles.

Whatever she had communicated, it seemed to do the trick. Immediately the black surface cracked open, revealing the hangar within. Zachary piloted the sledge inside and found an empty docking space on which to land.

"Welcome to the Fringg Galaxy Void Market," a robotic voice intoned over the lang-link. "We are not liable for any of the products or services supplied here."

It was the same way they'd been greeted on their last visit. The four departed through the sledge's door and walked toward the hangar exit, where a multiarmed outerverse being manned a security checkpoint.

"Please proceed," the alien said.

Zachary and Kaylee led the group onto the automated walkway that moved through a short, darkened tunnel before arriving at a tinted sliding door. When no beeps or alarms sounded, the alien cleared them, granting the group passage into the void market.

Upon entering, Zachary found it to be even rowdier and more boisterous than the last time he was there. The eight-story-tall space station was teeming with illicit activity, none more pronounced than the bareback greebock-riding taking place inside the fenced-in ring on the ground floor. It was like watching a bucking bronco at the rodeo, except the greebock was the size of a bison, and with every kick of its hooves, it let out a trumpeting growl that shook the whole room.

A thin, limber creature with long wooden arms and legs that made it resemble a stick bug was desperately clinging to the beast's back. Many of the spectators gathered around the balconies above the ring cheered and hollered, but they reserved their biggest roar of approval for when the rider was thrown from the back of the greebock, somersaulting through the air and crashing down on the straw- and dirt-covered floor of the ring, directly in front of the enraged beast.

"I forgot what passed as entertainment here," Zachary said.

"And I forgot how sensitive you can be," Kaylee replied. "He'll be fine."

The greebock let out a snort and charged forward, trampling the delicate-limbed rider underfoot and sending splinters and wood chips everywhere.

"Okay, that might be a slightly longer road to recovery," Kaylee said, wincing.

A pair of custodial aux-bots rolled across the ring, sweeping up the scattered debris. A giant electronic board on the far wall illuminated a time of twenty-two seconds. It was added to the leader board, placing sixteenth, well behind the current first-place time of one minute and fifty seconds.

Zachary and his companions walked deeper into the void market, past the gambling tables, the neon tattoo parlor, and the wall of sleeping pods. No one gave them a second glance. In the void market, it was customary to mind your own business. They continued beyond the long counter, where an assortment of ruffians slurped sluglike creatures out of gigantic seashells, and arrived at an area where mechanical parts were being traded.

"Skold's contact—I think her name was Tatania—should be holed up at one of these," Zachary said, surveying the surrounding booths. Then he spotted her: a willowy female figure with sandpaper skin and two human-sized amoeba guards flanking her.

Zachary led the way, right up to the table where she sat counting serendibite. The guards reached out their appendages to stop him from coming any closer. One of them made a strange bubbling sound from within, and Tatania looked up.

"I'm busy," she said, quickly turning her attention back to the clear cubes laid out before her. But then she glanced up again. "Wait. I remember you. You're the ones Skold tried to pawn off on me for a single bound of fuel."

"Yes," Zachary said. "That's why we're here. To see if he's been in contact with you. Or if you have any idea where we can find him."

"You're not the first to come asking," Tatania said. "The question is, why should I tell you?"

"We can pay," Ryic answered.

"Everyone can pay," Tatania replied. "I just haven't received an offer that seemed worth it yet." She was about to dismiss them again when a smile crossed her face. "There is something else I want, though. A favor. You might have seen that bucking greebock on your way in. The individual currently in first place rides for one of my business competitors. The bragging rights that go to the ultimate winner . . . well, you can't really put a price on that."

"I'll ride," Kaylee volunteered.

"No," Tatania said. "I'm not interested in you." Her eyes turned to Ryic. "I want the Klenarogian."

"Me?" Ryic asked.

"You should know," Tatania replied. "Your people are born riders. All the intergalactic record holders hail from your planet. Those elastic limbs give you a real advantage."

Ryic was already shaking his head.

"You'll be fine," Kaylee said. "She's right, you were born for this."

"I don't like being in the spotlight," Ryic said. "And I don't like getting trampled even more."

"We wouldn't ask if we had another option," Quee said.

Ryic let out a nervous sigh. "Fine. I'll do it."

"Are you sure?" Zachary asked. "Didn't you see what happened to that stick bug thing?"

"Let's get it over with before I change my mind," Ryic said.

Tatania stepped out from the booth and took Ryic's hand. "And I thought it would be just another dull day."

"Now, hold on," Zachary said before they went any further. "How can we be sure you actually know where Skold is?"

"Because he was here not too long ago, asking if I could get him an atmospheric adapter," Tatania said. "Seems our mutual friend has retired and bought himself his own moon."

"What good does that do us?" Kaylee asked.

"I made sure there was a tracking device built into the

adapter," Tatania said. She turned back to Ryic. "And after you do your part, I'll tell you where to find him."

She led Ryic and the others into a tunnel below the ground floor spectator stands. They continued past a large stable, where a half dozen greebock were being fed and groomed. Tatania stopped before a table where a squat, fur-covered alien sat minding a sign-up sheet.

"I've got a late entry," Tatania said, handing over a cube of serendibite.

"This guy?" the alien asked, looking at Ryic.

Tatania nodded.

The alien shrugged and called out to one of the stable hands. "Sharpen up Grizz's horns. He's getting another ride."

Ryic's face was already reading regret, but he sucked it up and tried to put on a brave front.

"Come with me," the alien said to Ryic. Then he turned to Zachary and the others. "You can meet him back here after he's finished. Or sign for what's left of him."

Zachary could only watch as Ryic was led into a holding pen. He gave him an encouraging thumbs-up before exiting the tunnel with the rest of the group. When they emerged, they were ringside, standing with a crowd of onlookers. Zachary noticed that Tatania was staring up at a wrinkled humanoid with walruslike tusks, sitting in a private, roped-off mezzanine with a clear view of the ring.

"Your competitor?" Zachary asked.

"I know how much this means to him," Tatania replied. "That's why it's so important to me that he loses."

A bell sounded and a gate shot open. Grizz, the giant greebock, emerged with Ryic on his back. He only took four steps before beginning to kick his legs in a vicious attempt to throw the rider clutching at his mane. The impact of the beast's bucking hindquarters sent Ryic tumbling forward so that he was hanging upside down between the greebock's horns, staring directly into his face. Ryic's flexible arms held taut as he was jostled from side to side, rubbing his cheeks against the snarling beast's wet mouth. The crowd was on its feet, smelling blood. But Ryic made a miraculous recovery, tugging himself up over the greebock's head and securely onto his back.

Zachary glanced up at the giant electronic billboard and saw the clock cross the one-minute mark. He turned to Tatania and saw that she was keeping one eye on the ring and the other on her competitor, who was starting to inch forward in his seat.

Back in the ring, the greebock was taking a different tack in order to dislodge Ryic. He was running along the outer fence, leaning his side up against the rusted metal. Ryic was forced to swing both of his legs over the opposite side of the greebock to keep from getting dismembered. The clock was ticking past one minute and thirty seconds now, and Zachary was starting to think Ryic just might pull this off. It looked as if the walrus-tusked creature sitting in the mezzanine was fearing the same thing, as he was slipping a small device out from his pocket and inserting it into his mouth.

"What's he doing?" Zachary asked Tatania.

She glanced up and bristled. "That lousy cheat. He's got a greebock whistle. It'll send that beast into a fit."

Zachary thought fast, removing his retracted warp glove from his pocket and activating it. He took aim on Tatania's competitor, and with one fluid motion his arm reached into the warp hole, emerging inches from the walrus-tusked creature's mouth. He swiped at the greebok whistle, but the creature turned and blocked Zachary's glove with one of his ivory tusks. The creature glanced across the ring at Tatania and sneered as he prepared once more to blow the whistle. What he didn't account for was a second gloved hand thrusting out from a hole behind his head, taking ahold of the back of his skull, and slamming his face into the metal rail before him. The vicious blow knocked the whistle clean out of his mouth and over the edge of the balcony. Zachary turned to see Kaylee looking rather pleased with herself.

Ryic's arms were stretched like putty as his heels dragged along the ground, but he held fast. Then the crowd began to chant in unison, and although they were shouting in hundreds of different languages, it was clear that it was a countdown. Zachary could even make out a few of the English speakers: "Five . . . four . . . three . . . two . . . one!"

Zachary looked to the billboard and saw that the clock had passed one minute and fifty seconds. And it was still going. Kaylee and Quee celebrated, cheering for their friend. Tatania couldn't help but gloat, giving a none-too-subtle wave to her competitor, who still seemed a little disoriented from the face-plant Kaylee had given him. Tatania leaned over to Zachary and whispered.

"You can find Skold on the fourth moon of Ionary. Send him my best."

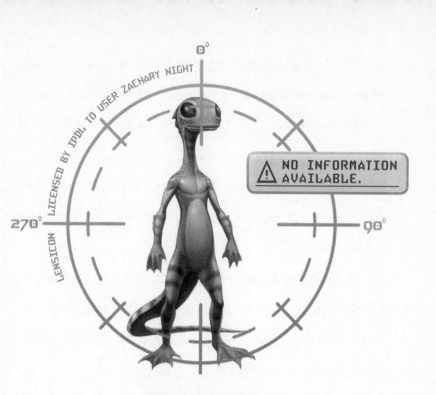

0°

270°

90°

⚠ NO INFORMATION
AVAILABLE.

«SEVEN»

"Four minutes and twenty-six seconds," Kaylee said. "You set a new record."

Ryic still looked traumatized from the experience. "*Someone* could have told me I had already won."

The sledge was three million miles away from the Fringg Galaxy, somewhere along its journey to the moons of Ionary. The Starbounders-in-training were sitting in the galley as the autopilot manned the flight deck.

"Well, if starbounding doesn't work out, you can always become a professional greebock rider," Quee said.

"You did awesome back there," Zachary said. "You should feel good about yourself."

"Pride is a decidedly human feeling," Ryic said. "For me, there is reward enough in knowing that I've done what is right—"

"Enough with the serious stuff," Kaylee interrupted. "Who's up for a little game to pass the time? Truth or dare, anyone?" The others just shrugged. "Great, I'll go first. Ask me anything."

"Do you like Zachary?" Quee asked, without missing a beat.

"Yeah, of course," Kaylee replied.

"No, not just as a friend," Quee said. "Do you really like him?"

Kaylee considered. "Dare."

Zachary did a double take. What did that mean? Why would she take the dare? Did she *like* him, like him, but was just too afraid or embarrassed to say so? Or did she think the truth would hurt his feelings?

"I dare you to eat this entire tube of anchovy spaste,"

Quee said, tossing it to Kaylee.

Kaylee grimaced, but she was never one to back down from a challenge. She unscrewed the top and brought it to her lips. After taking in its fishy odor, she paused. Maybe Zachary was going to get an answer after all. But then Kayle squeezed the tube and sucked down the spaste. Once she was finished, she eyed Quee.

"Okay, now it's your turn," Kaylee said. "What's the most illegal thing you've ever done?"

"Wow. There are so many to pick from," Quee said. "If I had to choose one, though, I'd probably say helping facilitate a plot to assassinate the minister of time travel." The rest of the group just sat there silently. "What? It wasn't successful."

"I've got one for Zachary," Ryic said excitedly. Everyone turned. "It's a toughie, though. So consider yourself warned." He took one last dramatic breath. "What's your middle name?"

Zachary smiled. "Frederick."

"No," Kaylee said, shaking her head. "That doesn't count. Ryic clearly doesn't know how to play this game."

"Seemed like a fair question to me," Zachary said.

"You need to take a dare to make things right," Kaylee said.

"Fine," Zachary said, playing along. "Hit me with your worst."

"I dare you to go in the ship's cryo freezer for sixty seconds."

"No problem."

"In your underwear."

Zachary wasn't going to let her get the satisfaction of seeing him flinch. So instead he started to undress. He quickly stripped down to his boxer shorts, and while his friends snickered, he opened the door to the four-by-four-foot freezer and marched himself through. Kaylee sealed it shut behind him. Stepping inside, he was immediately hit with a shock of stinging cold. His lungs tightened as the chilled air entered his chest. The skin under his fingernails turned an icy blue and he already felt like his toes might fall off. And he'd been in there for only about fifteen seconds.

Zachary had been taking an elective course at Indigo 8 called Extreme Survival, and one of the first classes was about learning how to deal with intense heat or cold. Now seemed like as good a time as any to put some of the lessons to use. *First tactic: train your mind to focus on a set point, thereby shifting attention away from the primary source of pain.* Zachary pinched the skin on his thigh, squeezing it between his thumb and forefinger until it turned bright red. *Second tactic: let yourself shiver to create extra body heat from the energy expended.* Zachary had no problem doing that, teeth chattering and limbs trembling. *Third tactic* (this was the strangest of all, but of utmost importance)*: sing to yourself.* So Zachary started humming "Twinkle, Twinkle, Little Star" out loud. There was no way he was going to admit to the others that he kind of wanted out right now. He'd stay in there no matter how numb he got.

His eyes wandered around the chamber, the seconds ticking by as if time had been frozen, too. In the corner, between canisters of oxygen and nitrogen, was a small metal table on wheels. A diamond-shaped creature with spindly legs was pinned down atop it. Zachary had never seen anything quite like it before. He moved a little closer to see that the creature's outer surface wasn't just sparkling because of the frost coating it. The entire organism seemed to be composed of a crystalline glass. Suddenly its long appendages sprang to life, clawing at Zachary. Zachary jumped back, and fortunately the straps binding the creature prevented it from leaping off the table.

Zachary was curious enough to take another step forward. But before he could, the door to the cryo freezer swung open and Kaylee reached in to grab his arm. She pulled him back into the galley.

"We thought you were dead," Kaylee said. "We've been knocking on that door for the last thirty seconds."

Ryic came over with Zachary's clothes and he quickly put them back on.

"I must have lost track of the time," he said, not letting on how frigid he felt.

"Was there a party in there?" Kaylee asked.

"No, but there is something else," Zachary replied. "I don't know what the Black Atom Society was using this sledge for, but they were keeping a souvenir on ice."

Just then, the sledge's automated communications system called out over the ship's intercom. "Lang-link request is being made by a nearby moon." The four of them departed the galley and returned to the flight deck. "Should I initiate connection?"

"Yeah, put it through," Zachary said.

The cockpit radio hummed to life, and this time a different computerized voice, one coming from off the sledge, spoke.

"Please state the reason you are trespassing in this orbit. You have entered private outerverse property. Without authorization, your ship will be terminated."

The complete lack of emotion in the voice only made the threat more ominous.

"This is Zachary Night of the earthbound IPDL training academy Indigo 8. I am looking for Skold Ota Stella. If his whereabouts are known on these Ionary moons, we request permission to land."

"Vocal patterns confirm identity, and tone and modulation indicates truthfulness. Permission granted."

Immediately the landing coordinates appeared on the sledge's starbox. Zachary and Kaylee took the pilot seats, while Ryic and Quee buckled in behind them. Once the young Starbounders had taken manual control of the sledge, they began to follow the newly displayed route toward a small moon that appeared to be showing only the earliest signs of life. Fields of light-green grass covered its surface, but there were no trees, forests, or jungles to speak of.

"Now we know what Skold needed that atmospheric adapter for," Ryic said. "He's creating a living, breathing planet on a dead moon."

As the sledge continued its descent, Zachary could see what looked like an enormous vacation resort come into view, with swimming pools and waterfalls, even a roller coaster track with hanging cars zipping along its rails.

"He built his very own amusement park," Kaylee added.

It appeared there was more under construction, too.

"Is that a ski mountain?" Zachary asked.

As they got closer, they could see a fresh coat of artificial snow getting poured on.

"He always said he wanted his own moon," Kaylee said. "Looks like he got it."

The sledge touched down on a freshly built concrete tarmac. The four exited the ship to find that the air was thin but breathable. They could hear what sounded like squeals of delight. Zachary glanced up at the roller coaster and spied a pair of orange-and-black amphibious humanoids raising their arms above their heads and screaming as the car they were in made a sudden dive down a steep drop. Zachary remembered them from his visit to Cratonis. They were Skold's kids.

Zachary, Kaylee, Ryic, and Quee headed for the palatial estate towering above the center of the grounds.

"Just how much did Skold get paid for that perpetual energy generator, anyway?" Ryic asked.

"Obviously a lot," Quee replied.

They hadn't even reached the front steps when the muscular, shaved-headed figure they had come to know as Skold exited through the door. Of course, this wasn't how the infamous alien fugitive actually appeared. The real Skold looked just like the one-foot-tall, web-footed creatures riding the roller coaster. This was just the robotic outer shell that allowed him to pass as human, and other than the grayish skin and unblinking eyes, it was entirely convincing.

"You're like a bad case of spacefluenza," Skold said. "I just can't seem to get rid of you."

"This is quite a place you've got here," Zachary said. "You must have sold a lot of used freighters to afford it."

"What exactly are you implying?" Skold asked innocently.

"We know you stole the perpetual energy generator," Kaylee said. "We watched you fly off with it. All of Callisto shut down. You nearly killed us."

"But you're here now, so I guess it worked out for everybody."

"What did you do with it?" Zachary asked. "Who did you sell it to?"

"I'm afraid the buyer insisted that I sign a confidentiality agreement."

"We think someone has attached it to a kinetic force sink and is using it to destroy suns," Zachary said.

"As in wiping entire planets from the outerverse," Kaylee added.

"I don't know anything about that," Skold said, the cold face of his carapace giving away nothing.

"We're not suggesting you do," Zachary said. "In fact, I'm naive enough to think even you would put the survival of billions of life-forms ahead of getting rich."

"Clearly you don't know me as well as you think you do."

"All it would take is one call to Indigo 8, and a hundred pitchforks would be surrounding this place within hours," Zachary said.

"So I'm a wanted man?" Skold asked.

"Yep. Full-on level-three bounty search," Zachary replied. "Madsen's got a file a hundred terabytes big on you. And don't think I wouldn't turn you in."

"That's a dangerous threat to be making when you're standing here unarmed on my moon."

"What did you let us land for if you weren't planning on helping us?" Kaylee asked.

"I was hoping to get some information on my criminal status. And you just gave it to me. Now that I know I'm a level three, I'll be sure not to set foot across the Indigo Divide."

Suddenly a voice called out from the doorway behind Skold in a series of squeaks and clicks. Zachary could see a long tail slithering across the floor, and by the way she seemed to be yelling at him, he figured this must be Skold's wife.

"Please, just let me handle this, dear," Skold said.

More clicks and squeaks.

Skold stopped speaking English and continued the heated argument in his native alien tongue. Back and forth they went, until Skold seemed browbeaten and defeated.

"Fine," he said. "I'll help you."

"Great," Zachary replied, wondering what exactly Skold's wife had said to convince him. "Do you want to give us a name or address? Or show us the way yourself?"

"Well, we can't do anything until sunrise," Skold said. "The galactic fold I used to bound to the location of the handoff opens only once a day. So I guess that means you're spending the night."

∘ ∘ ∘

It was, without a doubt, one of the strangest dinners Zachary had ever experienced. And it wasn't just the food, although the homemade mealworm lotus cups were practically crawling right off the plate. It was also the way Skold's wife chewed up the food and then spit the partially digested bits directly into her kids' mouths.

The experience was made stranger still by the fact that, while the estate was large enough to house a royal court, the furniture was doll-sized to accommodate the small stature of Skold's family. This forced Zachary and his companions to sit cross-legged on the floor, appearing as if they were giants in comparison.

On the bright side, conversation was aided by a sphere placed on the table, which served to translate the squeaks and clicks into English and the English into squeaks and clicks.

"What's it like being a Starbounder?" the older of the two young amphibious creatures asked, leaning forward on the edge of her seat.

"Take the thrill you were feeling on that roller coaster outside, and multiply it by a thousand," Kaylee said.

The girl's eyes went wide. "Do you think they'd accept someone like me?"

"It depends," Quee replied. "What can you do?"

The newtlike creature thought about it for a second, then shot her tongue across the table and around Quee's neck, tightening it like a noose.

"Yeah, you'd probably fit right in," Quee coughed out. "As long as you've got something unique to offer, it seems everybody's welcome. Heck, they took me. Now I feel like

I actually belong somewhere."

The creature released her tongue and it flew back into her mouth.

"I'm not sure what you said to Skold earlier to change his mind, but thank you," Zachary said to Skold's wife.

"I told him we're thieves, not murderers," she replied. "If there was a way to help prevent harm to our fellow brothers and sisters around the galaxy, it was our duty to do so." Then her friendly smile turned cold. "And once he's done helping you, you're going to get him immunity for his latest crime."

Zachary had been curious what this seemingly genteel creature saw in Skold, but now he realized that they weren't so different after all.

Meanwhile, Skold's youngest was throwing mealworms at Ryic, using his pale head as target practice. Ryic was trying to restrain himself, but he lost his patience and slammed his fist down on the table.

"Enough!" he hollered.

The child let out a loud wail and began sobbing uncontrollably. Zachary and Kaylee immediately turned their gaze on Ryic.

"What? Why are you looking at me like I'm the bad guy?" Ryic asked.

Skold's wife brought out dessert—a special family recipe for glazed crickets—and served the guests first. Skold glanced over at Zachary and Kaylee, who looked none too eager to indulge.

"Don't worry, they taste just like chocolate," he said.

Zachary took a bite. He wasn't sure what Skold was talking about, but this certainly didn't taste like any chocolate he had ever had.

The meal ended soon after, and Skold's wife led the four Starbounders to the guest quarters, where they were each shown to their own bedroom, furnished with beds far too small for them to sleep on. She provided them with blankets and pillows instead, but it didn't really matter, because once Zachary curled up on the floor, he was sleeping within minutes.

∘ ∘ ∘

Hours later, Zachary woke to find the sun streaming in through the blinds and Skold standing over him.

"Rise and shine," he said. "Time to get a move on. Unless you want to stay for breakfast."

Zachary was on his feet instantly, gathering up his friends and following Skold out the door. They headed back for the sledge, passing under the spiraling roller coaster and across some snowdrifts that blew in from the nearby mountain. Once they arrived at the ship, they quickly climbed on board and hurried to the flight deck.

"So, where are we going?" Kaylee asked, bringing up the Kepler cartograph.

"Where we're headed doesn't have a name," Skold said. "I do most of my business in those kinds of places. Places you can't find on a map. That's why I'm coming with you."

He made himself at home in the pilot seat and began moving his hands swiftly, lifting the sledge up from the tarmac for takeoff. Skold's ability to control a starship was inspiring, but knowing how many of them he had stolen, Zachary was hardly surprised he was so good at it. It wasn't long before the Ionary moons became distant dots and they were bounding through a galactic fold that didn't appear on the cartograph.

They came out straight into the middle of a geomagnetic tornado. Warning lights flashed and blared loudly. And although Zachary couldn't actually feel it, he could see out through the window that the sledge was being pulled in rapid circles.

"What are you trying to do, kill us?" Zachary asked.

"I already told you, when you make deals as illicit as the ones I do, you want to be sure it's in a place where nobody uninvited is going to crash the party."

"Well, the only ones who look like they're going to be crashing here are us," Kaylee said.

Billions of particles were slamming against the sledge's outer hull, like hail hitting a tin roof. The ship continued to spin, only faster now, as it was tugged sideways toward a black hole.

Suddenly Zachary noticed a small but perceptible change in everything around him. His companions and the sledge itself were starting to stretch, as if they were inside a funhouse mirror. This must have been what Ryic felt like on a daily basis. But rather than putting the engines in reverse and trying to pull the ship away from the monstrous vacuum, Skold waited for the centrifugal force to build and then slingshotted them away from the danger. The sledge emerged from the geomagnetic twister and glided through a calm expanse of space.

Zachary, sweat dripping from his brow and armpits wet, looked like he had just run at full speed on a treadmill. His friends appeared equally rattled.

"What's everyone so bent out of shape about?" Skold asked. "I do this all the time."

Skold activated the ship's standard radiation scanners, which illuminated a faint glowing trail in the distance.

"I handed off the generator not far from here," he said. "Looks like it left some bread crumbs to the next galactic fold."

Skold followed the trail as far as it would take him, but the end point was not a galactic fold. It was a ship.

"That's strange," Skold said, staring out at the lone dreadnought drifting slowly through space. "That's the ship I made the transfer on."

"So what's it still doing here?" Zachary asked.

0°

270°

90°

LIFE-FORM:
MOLKING RAIDERS
THIS OUTERVERSE SPECIES OF SPACE
PIRATE HAS NO ALLEGIANCE OR TIES TO
ANY KNOWN GOVERNMENT OR INTERPLAN-
ETARY COALITION.

«EIGHT»

As the sledge slowly approached the eerily still dreadnought, Zachary could see warning lights flashing inside the other ship's flight deck. Skold pulled up alongside the massive ship and slowed the sledge to a crawl.

"Please unlock your atrium. We wish to board your vessel," Skold said into the lang-link.

Zachary, Quee, Kaylee, and Ryic stood by, waiting

with Skold for a response. Only silence came in return.

"If you don't respond now, we will force our way in," Skold insisted angrily.

"Maybe they're sleeping," Ryic proposed. "I wouldn't run for the lang-link if I were all snuggly in my sleeping pod."

"They would have their auto-reply activated if that were the case," Kaylee said. "Either they're not interested in visitors or something is very wrong."

"Let's extend the O_2 bridge and have a look around for ourselves," Skold said as he floated out of the flight deck.

Zachary and the others followed, heading down to the exit portal. Through the glass window, they watched as a clear tube stretched from the sledge toward the exterior of the dreadnought. The small arms at the end of the O_2 bridge gripped the footholds of the docking portal and locked into place.

"You might want to arm yourselves, just in case," Skold said.

Zachary and his fellow trainees activated their warp gloves.

"I was thinking of something with a little more

firepower." A compartment in Skold's leg slid open, revealing a cache of handheld weapons. He handed Zachary a voltage slingshot and gave Quee and Kaylee ionic daggers. He pulled a sonic crossbow from his waist and charged it.

"What about me?" Ryic asked.

"You're more of a danger to yourself with a weapon," Skold said.

The five floated through the exit of the sledge and drifted toward the gray outer hull of the dreadnought to find its docking portal was still sealed tight.

Quee inserted her trusty cryptocard, a thin rectangular slip of metal with numbers scrolling across the outside edge, into a narrow opening beside the door.

"We're not the first ones to tamper with this airlock," Quee said.

She punched a coding sequence into the extended portion of the cryptocard and waited. After a moment the door began to move, but it ground to a halt before opening fully. Quee had no trouble getting through, but it was a tighter squeeze for the rest, especially Skold.

Once inside, Zachary had to adjust to the strobing

red flashes of the warning light and the foul odor wafting through the desolate hallways.

"I made the trade-off with my buyer in the passenger cabin," Skold said. "He was a real nasty-looking Basqalich with more serendibite than you'd find on a void market Jai-Gar table. There were two more bruisers in the flight deck and another two in the cargo hold."

Skold guided the others toward the cabin, with his sonic crossbow leading the way. As he propelled himself through the corridors of the ship, Zachary noticed photon cannon holes riddling the walls. Many of the lights had been shot out, and the deeper the group got, the darker it became.

Zachary blinked in sequence, activating his lensicon's infrared, and his view instantly changed. Suddenly the shadowy halls were bathed in a bright-green glow.

As the team crossed into the passenger cabin, Zachary could see everything more clearly, including a lifeless Basqalich floating limply in zero gravity. Zachary moved over for a closer view of the body and saw that its green-skinned chest had been shredded with sonic fire and one of its orange tusks had been blown clean off.

"Maybe he was resisting arrest," Kaylee said.

"Those wounds didn't come from any IPDL-issued firearm I've ever seen," Skold said. "Looks like a decibel grater to me."

"Only Molking raiders use those," Quee said.

If there were any doubts about Quee's theory, they were quickly put to rest when a snaggletoothed beast wearing metal armor floated into view.

Zachary turned his voltage slingshot toward it, but before he fired, he saw that the creature's tongue was hanging out of its mouth and its diamond-shaped eyes were rolled back in its head.

Zachary blinked, and his lensicon's heads-up display identified the creature.

LIFE-FORM: MOLKING RAIDER

THIS OUTERVERSE SPECIES OF SPACE PIRATES HAVE NO ALLEGIANCE OR TIES TO ANY KNOWN GOVERNMENT OR INTERPLANETARY COALITION.

AFTER THEIR HOME PLANET WAS DESTROYED DURING A CIVIL WAR, THE MOLKINGS BECAME A NOMADIC TRIBE, EVER IN SEARCH OF NEW TERRA ORBS TO

CALL THEIR OWN. COMPROMISE IS SEEN AS A SIGN
OF WEAKNESS, AND THE ONLY WAY THEY VIEW AN
ARGUMENT SETTLED IS WHEN ONE PARTY IS DEAD.

"I found two more members of the crew," Skold called out from the neighboring flight deck. "They're dead, too."

"If the perpetual generator is still on the ship, the only place it would be is the cargo hold," Zachary said, pushing himself toward the back of the dreadnought.

"I wouldn't hold your breath," Skold replied. "It looks like this place has been picked clean." He pointed to the rows of emptied underbins and the spots where circuit boards had been ripped out of the walls. "Molking raiders take everything."

"Why would they bother with scraps and wiring if they came for the generator?" Ryic asked.

"They're Molks," Skold said. "They can't help themselves. If it's not nailed down, they take it. And if it is nailed down, they take that, too."

Zachary, now moving alone, came to the open door of the cargo hold. He pulled himself inside and saw the large empty space where something had once been strapped down, but only the security webbing remained. He was about to head back for the main cabin when his eyes caught sight of a dead Basqalich stuck to the ceiling. Skold had said there were two crew members in the cargo hold. So where was the other?

Suddenly Zachary felt something grab his ankle. He looked down and had his answer. A Basqalich was weakly gripping his friction boot. The creature's skin was stained purple from the fluid still oozing out of its wounds.

It labored to speak but managed to get out a few words. Unfortunately, they were in an off-planet language that Zachary was unable to understand.

"*Og-weil-tbora,*" the Basqalich wheezed from its cracked lips.

"I don't understand you," Zachary said.

"*Ngro-non eh . . .*"

"Skold, get in here!" Zachary shouted. "One of them is alive."

The Basqalich was fading, its life draining from its face. The creature turned and began rubbing its finger along the metal wall, making lines of purple ooze. Zachary watched expectantly as letters formed.

IOIOIOIO

"What does that mean?" Zachary asked, half to the Basqalich and half to himself.

But he would not get a response. No one would. The creature was dead.

Skold and the others flew into the cargo hold with weapons drawn.

"It's too late," Zachary said.

Kaylee and Quee were already eyeing the markings on the wall.

"Io?" Kaylee asked. "That's Jupiter's moon. The one that the Callisto Space Station is hidden behind."

"Why would Basqalich traders be telling us to go there?" Ryic asked.

"They wouldn't," Quee replied. "It's not an *I* and an *O*, it's a one and a zero. It's binary code. The only universal language in the galaxy."

"What does it mean?" Zachary asked.

"In this context, I have no idea," she responded.

Zachary saw that Skold was jimmying open a secret compartment in the floor. Glass canisters filled with a green liquid were hidden inside.

"Nitro chargers," Skold said. "Any raider worth his salt never would have left here without finding these."

Skold pushed himself back out into the cabin.

"Where are you going?" Zachary asked.

Skold didn't answer. Zachary and his companions followed. When they caught up, Skold was examining the blast wounds covering the Molking raider's body.

"These are dry," Skold said. "The ones on the Basqalich are still relatively fresh. My guess is he was dead before he ever stepped foot on this ship. Someone brought him here to throw us off their scent. It was a setup. Molking raiders don't seem like the type who build star-killing devices, anyway."

"So somebody hires Basqalich middlemen to round up all the parts," Zachary said, "then kills them off and tries to make it look like Molking raiders are behind it. They really must have wanted to cover their tracks."

Quee pulled herself to the flight deck and zeroed in on the starbox. She jammed her ionic dagger into the equipment panel and popped it open. After a quick hack, she turned back to the others.

"They swept it clean," she said. "All communication

logs. Future destinations. Even the ship's manifest. Gone."

"There's a separate memory bank," Skold said. "It's built into the engine itself. It stores the coordinates of the last docked location."

"What good is that going to do us?" Ryic asked.

"Well, since we'll never know where this ship was headed next, we may as well find out where it came from," Skold replied.

Skold moved past Quee and removed a thin wire from the artificial flesh of his right wrist. He inserted it into the opening in the equipment panel and waited for the intended information to upload.

"Subquatica," he said. "A deep-sea tourist trap in the Tranquil Galaxies. The ship's arrival is time-stamped. If you want answers, you should go there."

"Aren't you coming with us?" Zachary asked.

"I already did my part," Skold replied. "You won't even have to take me home. I'll fly this."

"Um, guys, you're going to want to see this," Ryic said from the flight deck window.

Zachary and the others turned to look. Outside, the stars were spinning again and the ship was being swept into the pull of the black hole. It was the same one they had escaped from earlier, only now it had grown in both size and magnitude.

"On second thought, maybe I will join you," Skold said.

"We need to get back to the sledge," Quee said.

Skold retracted the wiring back into his arm, and the five rushed toward the dreadnought's docking portal, springboarding themselves through the corridors. Zachary caught a sideways glance out one of the ship's portholes and could see that the O_2 bridge was beginning to splinter. The sledge appeared as if it wanted to spin in one direction while the dreadnought spun in another. It wasn't clear how much time they had before the two would break apart completely.

The group reached the exit, and after Quee soared through, the others squeezed their way into the clear tube leading to their ship. Everyone but Skold, that is, whose broad shoulders got stuck in the narrow opening. What sounded like nails dragging across glass pierced Zachary's eardrums as the bridge was twisted like a piece of taffy. The noise nearly drowned out Skold's call for help, but Zachary turned. He doubled back and extended a hand to

Skold, attempting to pull him free.

Zachary heard a loud pop and saw where the first fissures had turned into a full-blown hole. Air was quickly being sucked out. Zachary gave one final yank and tugged Skold through. A long gash down Skold's right shoulder revealed the pistons and wiring beneath.

As oxygen continued to drain from the tube, Zachary and Skold hurried across. With every fraction of a second that passed, Zachary felt it getting harder to breathe. The hole in the bridge was growing and the suction was getting stronger.

Kaylee, Ryic, and Quee had safely passed through the entrance portal to the sledge. Although Zachary's fingers were beginning to lose their grip on the walls of the tunnel, Skold was right behind him, pushing him forward. The two reached the door and crossed inside, pulling it shut. As they did, the O_2 bridge snapped clean off, tumbling toward the void.

By the time Zachary reached the sledge's flight deck, Ryic was already in the pilot seat, starting the ship's engines. Kaylee had projected the Kepler cartograph onto the windshield and mapped out the fastest bounds to Subquatica.

"Get this thing moving," Skold said. "We don't have much time."

As Skold and Zachary buckled in, Ryic gestured to the control panel and the sledge lurched forward, directly toward the black hole.

"Turn around!" Skold shouted.

"I'm trying," Ryic replied.

Zachary unlatched Ryic's harness and pushed him aside.

"Don't worry, I got this," Zachary said.

He took the pilot seat and shifted the ship's direction, thrusting the sledge away from the looming cosmic vortex, leaving the dreadnought as the only space vessel the hole would be swallowing today.

Soon, they were soaring for the nearest fold.

"Why did you come back for me?" Skold asked Zachary.

"You were in trouble."

"You could have been killed," Skold said.

"Does that mean you'll come with us?" Zachary asked.

Skold looked out through one of the side windows and watched as the dreadnought began to crush in on itself.

"I guess I don't have much choice now," he said.

Zachary wasn't sure if Skold was referring to the fact that he no longer had a ship to fly himself home or that he now owed Zachary a favor. Either way, it appeared as though their team of four had become a team of five.

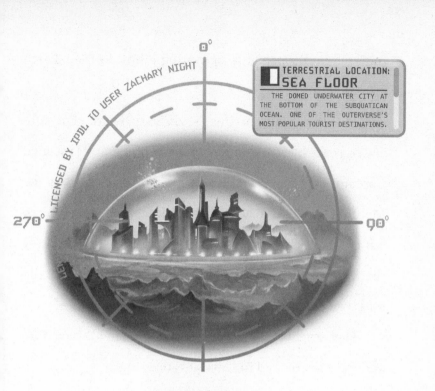

0°

270°   90°

TERRESTRIAL LOCATION:
SEA FLOOR
THE DOMED UNDERWATER CITY AT
THE BOTTOM OF THE SUBQUATICAN
OCEAN. ONE OF THE OUTERVERSE'S
MOST POPULAR TOURIST DESTINATIONS.

«NINE»

The flight to Subquatica was taking longer than anticipated, so the sledge was forced to stop at a remote fueling hub in the Crossroads region of the galaxy. While Skold negotiated a fair deal for a dozen fission canisters with the hub attendant, Zachary and the others discovered a lang-link in the docking station. Zachary sat before a small video screen displaying routing numbers to every IPDL base in the outerverse. He located the icon for

Indigo 8 and touched it, activating a link to their Earth base.

"Director Madsen, this is Zachary Night. I'm sure you're aware by now that Ryic, Kaylee, Quee, and I escaped Captain Aggoman's starjunk while it was docked at the Mammoths of Xero. I wish I could explain everything, but we can't risk compromising our mission. Just know that we're safe and doing everything we can to protect the outerverse. And please, don't come looking for us—"

"Hey, Zachary," Ryic interrupted, "we're all fueled up and the galactic fold to Kibarat is opening."

"Not now, Ryic!" Zachary shouted.

He quickly reached out his hand and terminated the lang-link. Once he was sure the message had been sent and delivered, he turned to Ryic.

"Perfect," he said.

"I don't know, you really think they'll believe I was stupid enough to blurt out where we were going right in the middle of the message?" Ryic asked. Kaylee's and Quee's looks said it all. "Don't answer that."

"If they do come searching for us, they'll be headed ten billion miles in the opposite direction," Zachary said.

Zachary felt they were making real progress, but he still knew that there were traitors intent on stopping them. Even within Indigo 8. They couldn't be too careful. Besides, he was getting used to going it alone, and they had made it this far just fine.

The four exited the booth and walked through the station. Even though it was a small port, it had a gravity anchor that simulated the pull of Earth perfectly. *It's nice to be walking for a change*, Zachary thought. They passed by a spaste shop filled with nothing but thousands of tubes, each bearing a picture of the flavor stored inside. Next door was a news portal, where holographic screens displayed live news feeds from around the outerverse. The group's attention was drawn to a particular story playing on over a dozen of the screens. Only one was in English.

"This is now the second star within the last forty-eight hours to be hit," a newscaster reported. "But unlike the attack on Protos, the sun of Clu 5 was completely extinguished, leaving its inhabitants in utter darkness. Evacuations are in progress, but the magnitude of these disasters is catastrophic."

"They're not going to stop at just two," Zachary said.

"We don't know that," Ryic replied feebly.

"The IPDL Security Council has put every available Starbounder on assignment," the newscaster continued. "Several high-ranking Clipsians, formerly under Nibiru's command, have been detained. But we want to stress that no one has taken responsibility yet for these attacks."

"You don't think we should tell Madsen what we know?" Ryic asked. "Think of all the manpower that's being wasted."

"We already know that somebody's working on the inside," Zachary said. "How else would those Basqalich bounty hunters have known that we were going to be on Adranus? Anyway, we don't need anyone else's help. We can finish this ourselves."

The trainees returned to the fueling hub, but Skold was nowhere to be seen. They looked around and called out his name before Quee finally spotted him on the opposite side of the station, sitting beside an aux-bot. As the group walked closer, they could see that Skold was having the damage to his shoulder fixed. Evidently the self-repair mechanism on his carapace couldn't quite match the precision of a maintenance robot.

"Not to rush you or anything, but suns are dying as we speak," Kaylee said.

"I know, I heard," Skold replied. "That's why you're going to want me in tip-top shape."

° ° °

Subquatica was a shining blue orb in space. Its entire surface was covered in ocean waters. Satellite beacons orbited the planet, guiding ships down to a giant artificial island with a landing pad on it. As the sledge slowly made its descent, Zachary could see that the waters were teeming with life. Pods of iridescent fish zigzagged just below the cresting waves. Gelatinous blobs with colorful tendrils carpeted swaths of sea.

The metal island was nothing more than long rectangles of steel used for takeoffs and landings. Zachary guided the sledge down, docking it between two clairvoyant observation ships.

"It's a popular tourist destination," Skold said. "Best underwater sightseeing in the outerverse."

The five disembarked and walked across the platform to a small building on the edge of the island with brightly painted pictures of fish covering the outside. Local Subquaticans, who looked like dolphins with legs and arms and gill-like folds on their temples, were there to welcome the visitors. One came up to Zachary and spoke in perfect English.

"Everyone here says they can show you around Subquatica," he said. "Sure, they'll take you to all the main attractions, but I'm the only one who will dive deeper into the secret realms. Come with me for just a few serendibite."

Zachary smiled but kept moving. He was pretty sure he could overhear every other guide there making the exact same promise.

They walked through the double doors to the building, and once inside saw passengers entering clear cylindrical vessels floating atop the water. As soon as the submersibles were filled, they would seal themselves shut and drop into the ocean.

"Well, they all look the same to me," Kaylee said.

Kaylee led the others into one of the undersea vehicles. A dozen seats were positioned around the outside ring of the glass bubble. Once everyone on board had strapped in, the doors locked and the vessel dipped below the water.

The view took Zachary's breath away, and it became instantly clear to him why so many traveled here to experience it. It wasn't just the fish and flora, but the water itself, which constantly shifted colors as the light from above caught it at different angles. It was like flying through a kaleidoscope, both dizzying and wonderful at the same time.

A voice spoke quietly from a speaker built into the headrest directly above Zachary's ear. "Welcome to *Nautilus One*, your underwater transport to the seafloor of Subquatica. During the trip, you might experience some increased pressure in your ears, so we've provided complimentary chewing gum in the armrests. Now, if you look to your right, you can see Subquatica's very own version of the sea horse."

Zachary turned to see a creature with a mane of yellow seaweed that waved and floated in the water, half galloping, half swimming right past his line of sight. He was so busy staring, it took him a moment to notice the school of suckerfish pressing their mouths up against the glass in front of Skold.

"And just a bit farther," the voice continued, "you'll

find the Coral Mountains, roughly the length of the Great Wall of China."

Zachary looked out at the enormous range of spiky orange stone branches extending well beyond where he could see. It seemed as if each seat was giving personally guided tours depending on the passenger's planet of origin. Zachary could barely make out the voice whispering to Ryic in what he assumed was Klenarogian.

The submersible continued its descent, the water growing darker the deeper they sank. "It seems we have an unexpected special treat for you today," Zachary's voice guide continued. "One of the largest Subquatican species, the boulder whale, is approaching. Please don't make any sudden motions. We don't want to aggravate it."

At first Zachary couldn't see anything, except for a giant shadow advancing toward them. But when the shape of the creature fully came into view, Zachary could see why it was called the boulder whale—it was *huge*. It had small, stubby legs that reminded him of a hippopotamus's, but the behemoth swam gracefully, getting frighteningly close to their vessel. Every passenger on board appeared to be just as much in awe as he was, their faces pressed up against the glass, staring out.

The submersible moved in for an even closer look, but apparently got a little too close, grazing up against the beast's nose. Even though it was just a gentle tap, the boulder whale didn't look happy. It opened its mouth and let out a gurgling roar. The vessel attempted to make a fast retreat, heading in the opposite direction, but the angry whale followed. As it closed in on them in what could only be described as attack mode, some of the passengers let out terrified screams.

Zachary kept his cool. He knew that they made these trips a thousand times a day. Surely they would have outrun a boulder whale before. But when Zachary looked back, he hardly had time to wonder if maybe he was wrong before the creature had expanded its jaw and swallowed the submersible whole.

The screams inside the vessel escalated into panic. As the whale's maw closed shut, everything went completely black. Zachary quickly came up with a game plan in his head. He'd arm himself with Skold's sonic crossbow and use his warp glove to blast a hole through the soft underbelly of the beast. But before he could act, there was a series of blinding flashes and then the whale opened its mouth and deposited the submersible into the entrance of an entire underwater city.

"Welcome to Sea Floor," the voice said above Zachary's ear, "the hub to all of Subquatica's destinations. If you'd like a commemorative photo from your trip inside that boulder whale, please pick one up at the gift shop."

Zachary suddenly realized that the entire incident with the whale had been a setup. The passengers around him were making the same realization, laughing to themselves. But there was one person who did not seem amused: Kaylee.

"You know how close I was to stabbing this ionic dagger through that whale's eye socket?" she asked. "Way too close."

"I suppose I could have warned you," Skold said. "But then I wouldn't have been able to watch you squirm."

Their vessel pulled into a tube at the front of the domed underwater city and came to a stop. The glass door of the submersible opened and all the passengers exited onto the platform. Several headed for the nearby gift shop, where pictures from the whale scare were popping up with each newly arriving vehicle.

Zachary looked out at the tall buildings stretching to the top of the dome. Treelined streets were populated with local Subquaticans manning storefronts and kiosks, hawking souvenirs to anyone who would stop. They wore colorful shirts with slits in the back for their dorsal fins and Bermuda shorts that their tails poked through. Small electric vehicles silently pulled up to the curb, picking up and dropping off tourists.

"Looks like there are security cameras covering all the exits and entrances," Quee said. "We know when the dreadnought arrived. I'll scan the footage and see if I can't find where the Basqalich went from here."

She led the group to a circuit box at the base of one of the cameras. With the others acting as cover, she knelt down and slid her cryptocard between some wires. It wasn't long before she was back on her feet, moving to a more discreet location to go to work. She accessed the feed from the time that had been stamped on the ship engine's memory bank and watched as footage played on the edge of the cryptocard. A few minutes passed quickly, then Quee paused the frame and rewound the footage.

"I think that's him," she said. "He looks a little differ-ent alive, though."

Skold came over to confirm it. "That's him, all right."

They continued to watch as the Basqalich waved down one of the electric cars at the curb. It had a green circle on the passenger door.

"Zoom in on the vehicle's identification number," Skold said. Quee froze the frame and enlarged the image. There on the back of the car was a seven-digit number. "It's a Green Dot, one of the cab companies duking it out down here. We'll pay them a visit and find out where our friend got dropped off."

The five hurried to the curb and flagged down the next available ride, a slick six-seater. A Subquatican spun his head around as the group climbed in, the gill-like folds on his temples making soft flapping noises as he breathed in and out.

"Where to?" he asked.

"Green Dot Cab Company," Skold replied.

"Of all the sights to see, it wouldn't have been my first recommendation. But the meter's running either way."

The cab zipped off, smoothly moving into the flow

of traffic. Zachary looked up through the open sunroof and saw fish swimming above the ceiling of the dome. It reminded him of when he'd lie in his backyard, watching birds fly overhead, and he wondered if kids growing up here would find that sight as strange as he found this one.

Each time the car stopped at an intersection, a different Subquatican would run up to the windows, flashing digital postcards and key chains in the shape of boulder whales.

"First time visiting?" the cab driver asked.

"For most of us," Zachary replied.

"Name's Sy. You got any questions, don't hesitate to ask. And don't hesitate to tip." He gave a friendly laugh. "Subquatica was built over two hundred years ago, for the tourists, of course. It's also become a hub of scientific research. There are only a few places in the outerverse where you can simulate the conditions we have naturally down here."

"Where did your species live before the dome went up?" Kaylee asked.

"Same place they still do. Out there, at the foot of the Coral Mountains." Sy pointed past the edge of the glass bubble. Zachary could see small underwater cottages. Outside of them, Subquatican children played and swam.

Suddenly the cab was slowing to a crawl. Cars were backed up for a mile. Up ahead, traffic was being detoured down a side alley.

"Looks like the Changing Tide parade started early today," Sy said. "I was hoping we'd beat it."

Up ahead floats with colorful streamers were spraying water into the adoring crowd of tourists lining the streets, as symphony music was pumped out from nearby speakers.

"They do this four times a day," Sy explained. "It's a celebration of our ever-shifting sea."

"More like another opportunity to separate these poor saps from their serendibite," Kaylee said, watching vendors pushing carts overflowing with trinkets and tchotchkes up and down the street.

The car turned down the alley and soon pulled up in front of a large outdoor lot filled with parked Green Dot cabs. There was a dispatch office out front. Zachary and Skold exited the car, while the others waited inside.

"We won't be long," Skold said to Sy.

Zachary and Skold entered the office and found an overweight Subquatican manning the front desk. He looked up and saw the odd pair standing before him.

"You know, most of our customers just *call* for a cab," he said.

"Actually, we need some information about where one of your cars took a passenger a few weeks ago," Zachary said.

"Can't help you," the Subquatican said. "That's confidential—" Skold had his sonic crossbow pressed into the creature's throat before he got out the last syllable. "Of course, everything's negotiable. Date and time?"

Zachary slid over a piece of paper with the vehicle's seven-digit ID number written on it, along with the approximate time of the fare. The Subquatican began tapping away at the keyboard of his handheld log.

"Here it is. The cab made a stop at the Research Quad, High-Pressure Center."

Skold dropped a cube of serendibite on the front desk.

"Keep this between us," he said.

"Not a problem."

Zachary and Skold shuffled out the door and climbed into the car.

"Research Quad, High-Pressure Center," Skold said to Sy.

"Something tells me you're not here on a sightseeing tour," he replied.

"Just drive," Skold said.

It was only a short trip to the four long, flat buildings, which hugged a portion of the dome. The cab came to a stop in the circular driveway outside. Skold and the young Starbounders exited.

"Wait here," Skold instructed Sy.

They headed for the closest building, which conveniently had a metallic sign hanging above its entrance that read HIGH-PRESSURE CENTER. The group walked inside, expecting to find many small laboratories, but instead there was just a single one that took up the entirety of the huge room. A handful of scientists, each a different species, was at work. One of them, a tall figure with long arms that reached down to her feet, approached Zachary and his companions.

"Are you the visiting scientists from the Milky Way?"

she asked. "We weren't expecting you until tomorrow. And we thought you'd be a little . . . older."

"No, we're with the IPDL," Zachary said. "We were hoping you might remember someone who came here a few weeks ago."

Quee walked up and flashed an image of the Basqalich on her wrist tablet. The figure took a long look, then shook her head.

"I'm sorry. I don't recognize him." She turned to one of the other researchers, a short, peculiar creature wearing protective gloves and safety goggles. "Hoff, come look at this."

The creature walked over and removed his goggles, revealing beady little eyes. Quee showed him the picture.

"Yes, of course," Hoff said in a lilting, almost musical voice. "I arranged to give him a magnitude modulator in exchange for a very generous grant."

"A magnitude modulator," Kaylee repeated. "What exactly does that do?"

"It's like a dimmer on a light switch, except it works on any power source," Hoff replied. "I was told it was going to be used for a planetary irrigation system, to make sure the appropriate amount of water got to each vegetative area."

"Well, I think you might have been deceived," Zachary said. "We have reason to believe that the modulator you provided is an integral piece of a star-killing device that was used to destroy the suns of Protos and Clu 5."

Hoff took a moment to consider the severity of what Zachary was suggesting.

"If someone were to combine a kinetic force sink, a perpetual energy generator, and a magnitude modulator, would they be capable of doing something like that?" Zachary asked.

"Yes, I suppose they would," Hoff said. "But only stars of a very specific size would be vulnerable. Too big a star, and the device wouldn't be able to absorb all the energy. Too small a star, and the device would have to get too close to the surface and risk melting. Take the suns of Protos and Clu 5. They're almost the exact same diameter and temperature."

"How many other suns are the same size and temperature as those?" Ryic asked.

"There's a simple way to find out," Hoff answered. He led the group to a computer set up at one of the lab's work stations and began typing. "In the known outerverse, only four: Arbez, Lemeck, R-21, and Opus Verdana."

Ryic was pale to begin with, but he turned positively cold. "Opus Verdana? That's Klenarog's sun."

"You're sure?" Zachary asked Hoff.

"Yes," the creature replied. "Every one of those suns—"

Suddenly one of the large windows behind them shattered and Hoff collapsed, a spray of sonic fire cutting him down. Skold and the Starbounders instantly dived to the floor, taking cover. Zachary couldn't see where the attack was coming from outside, but knew he and the others would be next if they didn't move fast.

A second volley of blasts tore through the lab as the scientists ducked under their desks and worktables. All around Zachary, laboratory equipment was being shot to pieces.

"They must have been watching the Quad," Zachary said. "Waiting for someone like us to come asking questions."

"Well, we're sitting ducks in here," Skold replied, crawling toward the exit.

The others followed behind as more bursts came

hailing overhead. Once they made it to the door, Skold held up a hand and stopped them. He reached into the utility compartment built into his carapace and pulled out four sticky spheres, which he used to scan Zachary, Ryic, Kaylee, and Quee. With four flicks of his wrist, he scattered them outside.

"Explosives?" Kaylee asked.

"No," Skold answered. "Doppelform projectors."

He pressed a button on a handheld device and holographic doppelgangers of Zachary, Ryic, Kaylee, and Quee ran out of the High-Pressure Center. Immediately an assault rained down from the window of one of the neighboring buildings, but the sonic fire shot straight through the doppelforms, leaving the dirt ground covered in holes.

Zachary looked to the circular driveway, but the cab was gone.

"On my signal, we run for that grove of trees," Skold said. "Now!"

The five sprinted, Skold running backward and shooting his sonic crossbow at the source of the sniper fire. He hit a figure in the window, sending it falling three stories. But it wasn't alone. Another shower of sonic bolts blew past the young Starbounders. They were halfway to the trees when Sy's electric car zipped out from between two of the Quad's other buildings, squealing to a stop in front of them. Zachary and his companions quickly piled in, and the cab was moving before the doors were even shut. More beams ricocheted off the outside of the car as it sped off.

"You stayed?" Zachary asked.

"I never leave a fare behind," Sy replied. The Subquatican seemed to be enjoying himself. "Anyone want to tell me what's going on?"

"We're still trying to figure that out ourselves," Kaylee replied.

"Get us back to the shuttle station as fast as you can," Skold said.

Zachary looked over his shoulder to see that they were now being pursued by a silver car, its windows tinted with blacked-out panes. Sy was weaving around cars, blowing through intersections, and nearly running down any pedestrian or street peddler in his way.

Skold took one window and Zachary the other, each reaching their arms out and firing in unison. Sonic blasts and electrically charged ammo hit the front window of the silver car but bounced right off without even making a dent. Zachary watched as a debris cannon emerged from the car's roof, launching a steel brick at them. It hit the cab's fender, sending everyone inside tumbling. Sy kept a firm grip on the wheel.

"Ten years I've been driving this cab," he said. "Never had a scratch on it!"

He made a sharp turn, cutting across four lanes of traffic and onto a pedestrian walkway. The silver car barreled after them. Zachary looked back once more, and while he couldn't see past the blackened windshield, it wouldn't matter for what he was about to do. He opened up a hole with his warp glove and reached into it. When his hand came out the other side, it was in the silver car. He blindly flailed around until his fingers found the wheel. Once he grabbed ahold, he gave a tug, sending the pursuing vehicle spinning into a guardrail. Zachary jerked his hand back just in time. The cab sped away, leaving the silver car in a smoking heap. Sy turned off the walkway and back onto the street.

"We need to go back and see who was chasing us," Zachary said.

"Are you crazy?" Ryic asked. "We need to get to a lang-link and contact the IPDL. Klenarog's sun could be next!"

"Even if we warn them, what can they really do?" Zachary asked. "We have the best chance of protecting Klenarog by stopping whoever's behind all this."

"That's my home planet in danger!" Ryic shouted back.

"The entire outerverse is in danger," Zachary countered. "You have to trust me."

"Hey, not to interrupt, but what do you want me to do here?" Sy asked.

"Turn around," Zachary said.

But that wasn't going to be necessary. The silver car had already recovered from the crash and was accelerating toward them.

"Maybe I should pull that warp glove trick again," Zachary said.

"You're not going to have time," Sy replied. "I'm afraid your ride ends here."

Ahead, the Changing Tides parade had brought traffic to a standstill, and there were no alleyways to turn down. For a mile to the left, right, and behind, cars were backed up. Skold handed Sy a handful of serendibite cubes, and he and the Starbounders jumped out and began running between cars toward the colorful floats.

They tried to blend in with the throngs of Subquatican peddlers and eager tourists. Zachary didn't have to look back to know that they were being followed on foot. The sound of people screaming was a dead giveaway.

Zachary glanced over his shoulder to see the crowd parting. Parade-goers were either running out of the way or being pushed. Once the mass had cleared, their pursuers came into view. But the figures weren't human or alien. In fact, they weren't living at all.

They were robots.

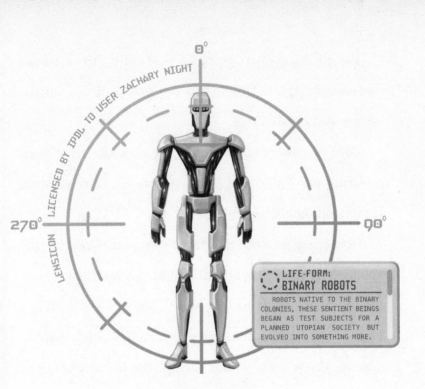

0°

270°

90°

LIFE-FORM:
BINARY ROBOTS

ROBOTS NATIVE TO THE BINARY COLONIES, THESE SENTIENT BEINGS BEGAN AS TEST SUBJECTS FOR A PLANNED UTOPIAN SOCIETY BUT EVOLVED INTO SOMETHING MORE.

«TEN»

There were two of them. Each was eight feet tall and solid metal, with two arms and two legs. Their faces had no mouths or noses, just a row of eyes down the center. Both held weapons in hand and stomped methodically forward.

"Robots?" Zachary questioned.

"From the Binary Colonies, by the looks of them," Skold said.

Blending in wasn't going so well. The pair of robots had already spotted them. So the group picked up the pace and started to run.

"That's what the ones and zeroes must have been referring to," Quee said. "Binary robots. They were on that dreadnought."

The group pushed and shoved its way through, but the robots were marching speedily right behind them.

"Why are we running away?" Kaylee asked. "We've been searching the outerverse looking for who's responsible and now we've found them. This is our chance to finally get some answers."

"How?" Zachary asked. "They don't look like the cooperative types."

"And they don't crack under interrogation," Skold added. "They have no emotions. They feel no pain. Not a lot of leverage to work with."

"But they have memory cards," Quee said. "They can be hacked, just like anything else made of wires and circuits."

"That would mean we'd need to disable one of them first," Ryic said.

Zachary got an idea. He eyed the parade floats and paid special attention to one designed in the shape of a whale, sending sprays of water from its blowhole. He spied a costumed Subquatican manning the float's portable hose and broke away from the others, hurrying toward it.

"Zachary, where are you going?" Kaylee called out.

"Cover me," he shouted back.

Zachary plowed through the dense crowd, maneuvering all the way to the front. Once there, he made a running leap onto the back of the whale float. A pair of local crowd-control officers tried to pull him down, but Zachary kicked them aside and scaled farther up the violet flower petals making up the big blue whale's back. The costumed Subquatican turned to see him.

"Hey, buddy, nobody's allowed up here," he said.

"IPDL security threat," Zachary replied, flashing his warp glove. "I just need that hose." He grabbed it out of the Subquatican's hand and aimed it at the two robots. "Turn this up as high as it goes."

The Subquatican twisted a valve and a massive jet of water exploded from the nozzle. It soared over countless parade-goers' heads and made contact with the robots' copper exteriors. The direct blast knocked the pair from their feet and caused both of them to short-circuit.

Zachary dropped the hose and leaped down to the ground. He caught back up with Skold and his fellow Starbounders, who were already rushing to the robots' sides. Despite the strange scene they had made, the parade continued on and most of the crowd had no idea what the brief commotion was even about.

"Nice work," Skold said.

"Thanks," Zachary replied. Then he turned to Quee. "You were saying something about hacking anything with a wire or a circuit?"

"The Binary robots are sentient beings," Ryic said. "It's not like taking apart a toaster."

"It's not so different, either," Quee said. "They may have evolved to have their own thoughts, but they still have to follow their internal protocol. The same way living organisms can't control whether they breathe or when their hearts beat, robots are still programmed to carry out their orders."

"Well, it seems like brainwashing to me," Ryic said.

"Don't worry," Quee said. "I'll be gentle."

Quee approached one of the robots and began unscrewing a small panel covering its neck.

"What are you doing?" Zachary asked.

"First, I'm going to wipe the termination order it was given," Quee replied. "Then I'm going to reboot its outer-verse positioning system so it takes us back to the location where it received it."

Quee dug her fingers deep into the nest of chips and resistors built into the Binary robot's neural cavity.

"Where'd you learn how to do that?" Skold asked.

"I used to practice on trash-bots in lower-tier Tenretni to get the inside track on where all the best precyclables could be found."

Quee tinkered some more, then removed her hands and put the panel in place. The Binary assassin quickly hummed back to life, rising to its feet and walking again.

"We better keep up," Quee said.

"What about the other one?" Zachary asked, eyeing the still-sparking bot on the ground.

"You fried its main board," Quee replied. "It won't be operational unless somebody gives it a total overhaul. And even then it'll have a permanent case of amnesia."

The reprogrammed Binary assassin was already charging ahead with what looked like singular determination. Zachary and the others hurried to catch up. It was as though the robot had no idea it was being followed. Zachary knew it would be faster to flag down a cab, but explaining why they were traveling with an eight-foot-tall robot just didn't seem worth the trouble. So they walked.

"I can't stop thinking about my home," Ryic said. "How everyone I know and care about is in danger."

"Try not to worry," Zachary said. "It won't do you any good."

"Easy for you to say," Ryic replied. "It's not Earth in peril this time."

"We're going to stop them," Zachary promised him.

"How can you be so sure?" Ryic asked. "We might have saved the outerverse once already . . . but a second time? I'm afraid you may be overestimating what you're capable of."

∘ ∘ ∘

It wasn't long before the robot was approaching the Sea Floor shuttle station, and it didn't stop moving until it reached one of the waiting submersibles. The doors slid open and Zachary and his companions followed the robot inside. They all buckled in, and the vehicle took off through the same tube in which it had arrived. The vessel rose up through the ocean much faster than it had descended, leaving the domed underwater city behind.

Once it had returned to the small building on the edge of the metal island, Zachary and the others exited the submersible and followed the Binary assassin back to the landing pad. The robot walked up to a pod-shaped sphere docked not far from their sledge.

"Should I go with?" Kaylee asked. "You know, to keep an eye on it."

"What if it takes us into hostile territory?" Zachary replied. "We're going to want to be together."

The Binary assassin boarded its ship, and the Starbounders and Skold quickly got onto theirs. As the sphere's engine began to glow awake, Zachary activated the sledge's camouflage shield, just in case they were about to be led into an enemy ambush. The two space-craft launched, and instantly they were flying into the cosmos.

Once they had left the atmosphere of Subquatica, Kaylee brought up the Kepler cartograph and identified the sphere's vehicular frequency, allowing the sledge to follow from a safe distance. They made several bounds through vast, empty portions of the outerverse before seeing any sign of civilization. But that sign, when it came, made for a most unusual sight. It appeared to Zachary as if the sledge had reached a glowing wall in space, one formed by a line of beacons stretching into infinity.

"It's a quarantine site," Skold said.

Ryic glanced at the Kepler cartograph, which showed that the ship was passing through the Olvang Nebula. "Scorpiositic fever," he said.

The others turned to him.

"Thirty years ago, a plague broke out on a small planet about fifty thousand miles from here. The virus started small, with microorganisms that caused only mild flu symptoms in their hosts. But rapid mutation and evolution enabled the organisms to grow exponentially larger, to the point where they were more like giant insects, able to survive on their own, devoid of any host. Rumor has it, they've gotten even bigger since then. That's why the IPDL built this galactic electron fence. To make sure no one goes in, and nothing ever comes out. Every usable fold in this nebula has been cordoned off."

Zachary knew there was an impenetrable barrier between the sledge and whatever deadly creatures were being kept behind it, but that didn't make him any less eager to get as far away as possible. Luckily, the sphere seemed to have the same idea. It bounded through another fold, and the sledge did the same.

The ships continued to travel across the outerverse, until the sphere made one last bound that brought the two spacecraft into a place different from any Zachary had ever seen before. The planets here were not round but cubes, built entirely of metal.

"The Binary Colonies," Skold said.

The planets were linked by bands of steel that made the solar system almost look like the double helix of an enormous DNA model. Surrounding them were giant spacecraft that resembled free-floating pyramids.

Zachary focused in on one of them and blinked twice.

MASSIVE SPACECRAFT USED BY THE ROBOTS OF
BINARY TO SET UP REMOTE COLONIES IN DISTANT
REACHES OF THE OUTERVERSE.

WHILE THE MAJORITY OF THESE FULLY FUNCTIONAL
CITIES OPERATE UNDER THE PLANET'S STRICT OPEN-
SOURCE POLICY, A FEW ARE RUMORED TO BE PARTAKING
IN UNSANCTIONED RESEARCH AND DEVELOPMENT.

(AN INTRAPLANETARY INVESTIGATION IS CURRENTLY
UNDERWAY TO CONFIRM OR REFUTE THESE CLAIMS.)

The sphere made its descent, heading toward the perfectly flat surface of one of the planets. The numbers *1001001* were imprinted on the metallic floor. Zachary guided the sledge close behind, and soon both ships were soaring lower. Unlike many of the previous destinations they had visited, there was no tarmac or landing pad. Spacecraft dotted the cityscape like cars parked in a busy downtown metropolis. The sledge touched down beside a giant golden obelisk that towered above it like a skyscraper.

All around them, every structure appeared to be identical. It was a symphony of corners and right angles, each one composed of small cubes stacked one on top of the other. Zachary was reminded of the building blocks his younger sister had been obsessed with since she was three.

Zachary and Kaylee were the first to exit the ship. To their left and right, Binary robots walked around them without giving them a second glance. Zachary overheard snippets of conversation.

". . . gravity seems extra strong today . . ."

". . . the new planetary bridge seems like a waste of . . ."

". . . hear about the mandatory upload for the internal auditory system?"

"They all speak English?" Zachary asked, surprised.

"They were built by a team of scientists at Indigo 8," Skold replied, now standing behind Zachary.

Roads and sidewalks were one and the same, only no cars drove on them. Zachary's lensicon identified the surface as a quickway, which was an appropriate name, as the Binary robots propelled themselves across it with what looked like motorized roller skates that they wore on both their hands and their feet. It was a strange sight, but the incredibly high speeds they were able to travel were no joke. Some seemed to be going over a hundred miles per hour.

"Better than a skateboard," Zachary said.

"And a lot more dangerous," Ryic added. "They should at least be wearing helmets."

"Their heads *are* helmets," Kaylee said.

Fortunately, the robot they were following was making his journey on foot. Also fortunate was the fact that other species like themselves cohabited this colony, allowing Zachary and his companions to appear less conspicuous.

"Why would anything other than a robot want to live here?" Zachary asked.

"The Binary Colonies started as an experiment," Skold replied. "The IPDL built them as a prototype of what a perfect society could be. Organized and regimented, every day exactly the same as the last. They populated the colonies with robots as test subjects, and over time the robots began to adapt, becoming more intelligent. Once other species experienced the simplicity and order of this way of life, many stayed."

"Being just another dot on the grid hardly sounds like perfection to me," Kaylee said. "It sounds miserable."

Up ahead, the Binary assassin was heading for a packed square where dozens of other robots were lining up at a series of upload stations.

"Once it gets into that crowd, it's going to be impossible to tell it apart from the rest," Quee said.

Kaylee reached into her pocket and pulled out a stick of gum from the *Nautilus One*, the vessel that had taken them down to Subquatica's Sea Floor. She unwrapped it and popped it into her mouth.

"Really, gum?" Zachary asked. "Now?"

Kaylee chewed for a few seconds, then removed the wet and sticky wad. She used her warp glove to open a hole in space, then stuck her hand through. When it came out the other side, just inches behind the Binary assassin's back, she pressed the gum up against its metal exterior.

"That should make it a little easier," Kaylee said.

The robot slipped into the mass of copper metal, and it just might have gotten lost among the other robots had it not been for the purple glob that Kaylee had cleverly stuck to its back. Once it emerged on the other side of the square, the Binary assassin headed in the direction of another gathering spot.

"Speedwheels Version Eight-point-three. Available now," the automated kiosk called out. "Trade your previous-generation model for the latest in velocity travel."

Robots were lined up exchanging old sets of wheels for new ones. Once again, the Binary assassin didn't stop, continuing its march right past the kiosk and turning down a less populated pathway. Zachary and the others would have little risk of losing their target here, as it entered a cordoned-off construction zone.

Modified Binary robots, ones with four metal legs instead of two and steel reinforcements built into their arms, carried giant girders up a corkscrewing ramp that stretched into the sky. It looked to Zachary as if they were erecting a new bridge to a neighboring planet. There were more construction robots doing equally heavy lifting, all under the supervision of an off-planet foreman, a delicate-looking creature with pointy ears and round, cat-shaped eyes.

The Binary assassin stealthily moved through the site, keeping to the shadows so as not to be seen. Zachary and his companions followed as it headed toward a man-hole cover. The robot removed the cover and disappeared inside. When Zachary arrived, he found a ladder leading downward, and he could hear the clanking sound of the Binary assassin's feet hitting the metal rungs as it climbed lower.

Zachary, Kaylee, Ryic, Quee, and Skold took to the ladder and continued their pursuit. They descended down the vertical tube, deeper into the bowels of the planet, until the Binary assassin reached the bottom. As the robot walked through a dimly lit tunnel, Zachary and his companions dropped to the floor and kept their fair distance. Skold gripped his sonic crossbow and his finger hovered over the trigger.

"Why'd you decide to pull out your weapon now?" Ryic asked.

"Nothing good ever happens a hundred feet below ground," Skold replied.

They moved slowly and quietly down the same tunnel, stopping at the edge of an opening, where they were able to peer around and see a cavernous space filled with over a thousand Binary robots, all analyzing different holographic displays projected on Kepler cartographs. Instead of using chairs, the robots merely bent their knees in simulation of a sitting position.

The Binary assassin walked over to a group of robots collected at a table isolated from the others. One rose upon his arrival. While he appeared identical to the rest, this robot somehow seemed to carry himself taller.

"What is this place?" Zachary asked.

"Looks like their version of Cerebella," Quee replied. "Only instead of running a small base like Indigo 8, I'm guessing it runs the whole planet."

"Shhh," Skold said, pointing a finger in the direction of the Binary assassin. "I'm trying to project what they're saying."

Zachary noticed a speaker built into the thigh of Skold's carapace and could hear robotic voices talking.

"Did someone pay a visit to our friend in Subquatica?"

"I don't know."

"What do you mean, you don't know? Why have you returned, then?"

"I don't know."

"You were programmed with one directive. To observe

the High-Pressure Center and eliminate anyone who came to talk to the scientist. Where's your partner?"

"I don't know."

Zachary watched as the robot reached out and snapped open the Binary assassin's neckplate.

"This is about to go south in a hurry," Skold whispered.

"We can't leave now," Zachary replied. "We still don't have any answers."

"He's been tampered with," they heard the robotic voice say through the speaker. Zachary could see that the robot was now looking at the gum stuck to the Binary assassin's back. His eyes immediately darted up and began surveying the room. "Shut him down."

"But, Commander Keel . . . ," another voice said.

"Now."

The robot, the one they called Commander Keel, was on the move.

"I don't say it often, but Skold's right," Kaylee said. "We should go."

Zachary spun on his heels and led the retreat back to the ladder. The group ran through the tunnel, but when they arrived at the base of the vertical tube, the ladder was gone. They doubled back, only to be met by a dozen armed Binary robots. Skold and the Starbounders pulled their own weapons and stood their ground.

"There are many more of us than there are of you," a voice called out. The robots stepped aside and Commander Keel approached Zachary. Close up, Zachary could see that he appeared war-torn, more rugged than the rest. A belt of geigernades was strapped around his waist. "Zachary Night. I was wondering when I might finally meet you."

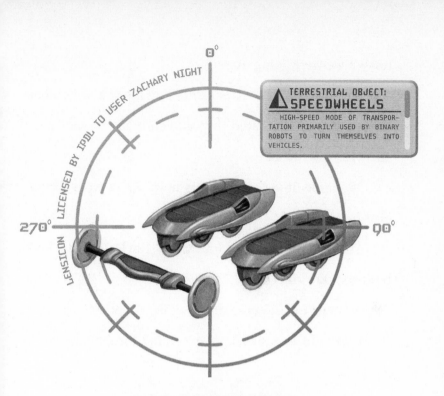

0°

270°

90°

TERRESTRIAL OBJECT:
SPEEDWHEELS

HIGH-SPEED MODE OF TRANSPOR-
TATION PRIMARILY USED BY BINARY
ROBOTS TO TURN THEMSELVES INTO
VEHICLES.

«ELEVEN»

"How do you know my name?" Zachary asked.

"I've been keeping tabs on you," Commander Keel replied, "ever since I discovered you were the last person to speak to Excelsius Olari before his death. Who do you think sent those Basqalich bounty hunters to Adranus to kill you and your friends when you started sticking your noses where they didn't belong?"

"That's impossible," Zachary said. "You couldn't have

known we were going there."

"On the contrary," Keel said. "Perhaps you remember the robot who facilitated the call you made to your parents? He was one of us."

Of course. It was so obvious now. There were robots everywhere.

"You're the one behind all this?" Kaylee asked. "You built the star-killer?"

"Not just me," Keel said. "All of us. Together."

"I thought this society was created to uphold order," Ryic said.

"That may have been the principle these colonies were founded upon, but we envision a different future now. One where robots are no longer made to do other people's bidding. This is our rebellion. Our chance to rise up against the living, breathing organisms that birthed us and then enslaved us."

"And you hope to accomplish that by eliminating a few sparsely populated planets?" Zachary asked.

"No, that's just the beginning," Keel replied. "We're going to destroy everything. The entire outerverse will fall. Now it's my turn to ask the questions. Who else knows you're here? Who have you told about this?"

"Nobody," Ryic said.

"He's lying," Zachary said. "The IPDL. Elite Corps officers are probably on their way now."

"What are you talking about?" Ryic asked.

Zachary gave him a sharp look, but it was too late.

"Tie them up," Keel ordered the other robots. "And find someone who can perform an extraction. We need to know if they're telling the truth."

Zachary and his fellow trainees lowered their weapons. Skold wouldn't give himself up that easily, though. He aimed his sonic crossbow, but before he got off a single shot, four robots pounced, pinning every one of his limbs to the floor.

The group was searched and had their warp gloves and weapons taken. Then they were led to a steel room with a slit in the wall no bigger than a four-by-six photograph. The robots departed, sealing the door shut behind them.

"There's no way we're leaving here alive," Zachary said. "They're going to pick us clean for everything we know, and as soon as they realize no one's coming for us, we're done for. So are those suns."

He kicked the wall so hard that he could feel his toes starting to bruise, even through the hardened tip of his friction boot.

"We wouldn't even be here if you had just listened to me," Ryic said. "But you think you're better than all the other Starbounders at Indigo 8, including us. Madsen was right. You are arrogant."

Zachary was about to protest, to defend himself. But he couldn't find the words. Partly because he knew his friend was right.

"What I want to know is why every one of those robots was staring at a Kepler cartograph when we walked in there," Quee said, changing the subject. "It looked like they were mapping every last galaxy in the outerverse. But if Hoff's theory was right, there are only four suns that are vulnerable. Why would they be studying the solar systems of every other sun?"

"He said this was just the beginning," Ryic interjected. "Maybe they're building a device capable of destroying larger suns."

Just then, the robotic voice of Commander Keel could be heard outside the window. "Operation Motherboard is a go." Zachary peeked through the slit and saw that Keel was addressing the entirety of the cavernous room over an intercom. "Thanks to our unexpected visitors, I've decided to accelerate our plans. Whatever final preparations were underway will have to be made en route. Go to your ships and fly to your assigned folds. Then stand by for further instructions."

The Binary robots shut down their Kepler cartographs and readjusted to standing position. They began to file out of the room, flocking en masse through a darkened archway in a far corner, leaving just thirty or forty robots behind. Commander Keel departed with the others.

"You think they're going after another sun?" Kaylee asked.

"Sounds that way to me," Zachary replied.

"But which one?" Skold asked.

Zachary continued to stare out the slit, this time eyeing their pile of confiscated stuff twenty yards away. Several Binary robots stood close by.

"I can see our warp gloves," Zachary said. "Now, if I only had mine, I could get it. Ryic, can your arms stretch that far?"

"I'm afraid that's a little out of my range."

Zachary turned to Skold. "How about you? You manage to sneak anything in here that could help us?"

"No, they stripped me clean. Even my utility compartment. Took everything but my carapace."

"That's it," Kaylee said. "You can climb right out that window and bring back one of our gloves."

"What?" Ryic asked. "He's bigger than all of us."

"The *real* Skold," Kaylee said.

Skold appeared a little disgruntled by the idea. "I prefer not to show that side of myself. Kind of bad for my tough-guy image. But I guess I don't have much choice."

"Mine's the purple-and-green one," Quee said. "Once I have my glove, I'll be able to hack into the security panel on the wall. Assuming my aim has improved."

Skold waited until the robots stationed beside the pile had dispersed. Zachary could hear gears shifting inside the suit, then Skold's chest cracked open and the two halves of his body split right down the middle, exposing the glass case where a black-and-orange newtlike creature sat. This was the real Skold. He looked just like his wife and kids, only somehow even cuter.

Skold popped open the door of the glass case and scurried to the floor. Kaylee knelt down beside him.

"Need a lift?" she asked.

Skold sighed. Humiliated, he crawled up her arm and she deposited him on the ledge of the narrow opening. Skold easily slipped through and made the four-and-a-half-foot leap down to the other side. He landed on the floor of the cavernous room with a thud but picked himself back up.

Without any of the remaining Binary robots seeing him, his tiny webbed feet ran all the way to the pile of weapons and he used his back to push Quee's retracted purple-and-green warp glove across the room. It was nearly as big as he was, and if it weren't such a dire situation, Zachary surely would have had a good laugh about it.

Skold was able to roll the baseball-sized orb up to the wall just below the steel room's window. Ryic reached through and stretched his arm down to the floor. He grabbed the glove and Skold and brought them both back into the cell.

"Any of you speak of this in the future, so help me, I'll hunt you down," Skold said. But his words were infinitely less threatening, coming from something resembling a classroom pet.

Skold darted into the glass case within the carapace and the exterior quickly locked back into place.

Ryic handed Quee her retracted warp glove and she activated it.

"Concentrate," Zachary said. "Remember what I showed you. It's just a soda can on a pile of rocks."

Quee gently spun her wrist, adjusted for distance, and opened a warp hole. She reached through and her hand came out the other side, directly in front of the security panel on the wall.

"Yes!" Quee said excitedly.

Using her cryptocard, she hacked the system, and after a moment Zachary heard a click inside the cell. Then the door slid open.

As they exited, Zachary spied a pair of Binary robots escorting a genteel-looking off-planet creature toward the steel room. She carried a satchel over her shoulder with dozens of needles sticking out from it.

"I think our extractor just arrived," Kaylee said.

Zachary surveyed the room. The remaining Binary

robots were scattered at their desks, and then there were the two additional robots walking in their direction with the extractor. The group's first priority was getting back their warp gloves and weapons, but the only way they could get to them was by walking right out into the open.

"Let me handle this," Quee whispered.

She didn't hesitate, ripping a hole in space. Her hand flew through to the other side and quickly rounded up the three remaining orbs.

"Now you're just showing off," Zachary said.

Quee struggled to get a grip, nearly bobbling one out of her palm. Once they were carefully balanced, she pulled them to her side. Zachary, Kaylee, and Ryic each grabbed theirs and slipped them on.

Zachary looked out to see the Binary robots and the extractor were nearing; it would be only moments before they were spotted. There was no time to retrieve the other weapons.

"We've got to follow Keel and that army," Zachary said, gesturing to the darkened archway through which the Binary robots had departed.

"Stop!" yelled out one of the Binary escorts to Zachary

and his gang. It pulled out a photon cannon and aimed. The first blast must have been a warning shot, as it struck just at Zachary's feet. He and the others sprinted for the archway as the deskbound robots turned, alerted to their presence by the cannon fire.

Kaylee was opening warp holes and using her glove to knock equipment to the floor to slow their pursuers. Quee reached through another warp hole of her own, attempting to grab one of their confiscated sonic crossbows from the pile but only managing to retrieve an ionic dagger.

Zachary, Skold, and Ryic were focused on getting to the archway, and once they did, Zachary saw where it led: a sloping tunnel stretching upward. The group began their ascent to the surface of 1001001, metal footsteps clanking behind them.

"We cannot terminate you without a kill order," one of the robots called. "But we will apprehend you by any means necessary."

A burst of photon fire struck the wall in front of the Starbounders, causing one of the support beams to snap. The ceiling above started to give way.

"They're trying to trap us!" Ryic shouted.

A second round of fire tore into the tunnel wall, further destabilizing the load-carrying beams. Zachary and the others raced under the crumbling debris as the tunnel collapsed. Without a forceful tug from Kaylee, Quee would have been squashed beneath ten thousand pounds of steel. The robots must not have anticipated that the group would be fast enough to escape, because now their plan had backfired. The collapsed tunnel had created a barricade between the robots and their prey.

Zachary exhaled. He could see the light shining in from outside. They were almost there.

Boom! Behind them, the blockade of fallen metal exploded as the Binary robots punched through. It seemed that this pursuit was not over yet.

Zachary and his companions reached the end of the tunnel and exited onto street level. They emerged in the courtyard of a derelict building that had been abandoned. Deep indentations in the ground and the footprints of scores of Binary robots made it clear that spacecraft had recently been parked here and the robots had boarded and departed on them. Zachary looked up and could see the glow of a hundred afterburners shooting toward a gizalith in the sky.

"We can still catch up," Kaylee said.

"But how do we get back to our ship?" Zachary asked.

"My internal compass is pointing that way." Skold gestured to a gate at the other side of the courtyard.

Zachary could hear the robots charging toward the foot of the tunnel. He and the others ran for the gate, sprinting across half a mile of cracked concrete.

They kicked open the iron door and found themselves in a busy trading bazaar. Spare arms and legs hung from hooks as robots in various states of disrepair hobbled about examining them. Zachary, Kaylee, Ryic, and Quee pushed through the marketplace, following Skold as he snaked toward a less congested thoroughfare.

Zachary looked over his shoulder to see the pursuing robots barreling their way into the bazaar and quickly scanning for their targets.

The locals minded their own business and neither helped nor hindered either side of the developing confrontation.

The robots were closing the gap between them. Zachary spied a bin of surplus metal craniums and started whipping them like dodgeballs at Commander Keel's oncoming soldiers. It distracted them for a moment, long enough to allow the group to bolt out from the bazaar and take to the street.

Skold's internal compass had directed them well. In the distance, Zachary could see the giant golden obelisk the sledge was parked beside.

"Out in the open we'll never stand a chance to outrun them," Ryic said.

"Who said anything about running?" Kaylee replied.

She was heading for the row of kiosks where the speed-wheels dangled on hooks. Kaylee grabbed what looked like a barbell with wheels and a pair of snap-on in-line skates. She watched some of the other robots gearing up around her and copied them, snapping her left and right feet into the skates, then dropping her hands to the ground as if doing a push-up. As soon as both her hands were planted firmly on the barbell, she zipped off at an alarming speed.

Zachary and the others were quick to follow, ripping speedwheels off the kiosk hooks.

"You know these are meant only for robots, right?" Ryic asked.

Zachary was immediately struck by how light the

barbell felt, given how bulky it appeared. He tossed the foot skates to the ground and stepped into them. The automated latches gripped his friction boots. He leaned down, and as soon as the handwheels touched the surface of the quickway, he was propelled forward. Zachary didn't have a moment to get used to the awkward position before he was immediately rocketing ahead.

Zachary knew how to ride a bike or a skateboard. But this was nothing like either of them. For starters, his face was just inches from the ground, meaning that any stray object in his path could leave him with a broken nose or worse. Then there was the steering, which was controlled by subtle shifts of weight and body stance. As for braking, well, he hadn't figured that out yet. Zachary just hoped he'd learn before he needed to come to a stop.

Ryic, Quee, and Skold were coming up alongside him, each with varying degrees of success maneuvering their speedwheels. Skold seemed like he was programmed for it, and maybe it had something to do with his carapace. Quee was also getting along fine. Ryic, on the other hand, struggled. His flexible form didn't appear well-attuned to this mode of travel, as his legs were stretching out behind him and nearly getting tangled into knots around even the slightest turns.

Zachary just tried to keep pace with Kaylee, who was skating toward the obelisk, where hopefully their sledge was still waiting.

"Right on our tail!" Skold shouted to the others.

Zachary glanced back and spied several of the Binary soldiers chasing them on speedwheels of their own. Clearly they were more experienced, which allowed them to weave effortlessly through the throngs of pedestrians and other quickway travelers.

Suddenly a kinetic blast struck Zachary's right-hand wheel, sending him so off-balance, he nearly collided with a steel wall. He looked back to see that it had been fired from one of the soldier's shoulder-mounted photon cannons.

"Isn't it a little risky to be firing at us like that without a kill order?" Zachary hollered back to the pursuing robot.

"Yes, it would be," the Binary soldier replied. "But the kill order was approved. Commander Keel has requested your termination."

It was hard enough to stay upright on the wheels

without dodging enemy fire. Another burst of concentrated light seared a hole in the elbow of Zachary's Starbounder jumpsuit. He tried to hug the ground even tighter to make himself as small a target as possible. The new position had the fortunate effect of speeding him up and bringing him side by side with Kaylee.

"I like the torn jumpsuit look," Kaylee remarked as she glanced in his direction. "Very rock star."

"You could have your own, if you're not careful," Zachary said as photon blasts zipped past them.

Up ahead, he eyed a quickway tube that seemed to be going in the direction of the obelisk but had a giant holographic red warning symbol posted in front of it: a picture of a set of speedwheels with a line through it.

"I'm sure there's a reason we shouldn't go in there," Kaylee said.

"With our luck, it's probably filled with explosives and dehydras," Zachary replied. They shared a smile and shifted their weights toward the tunnel.

Zachary was the first to enter, shooting straight through the holographic warning sign. He was pleasantly surprised to find it empty and easy to traverse.

"There's nothing in here," he called back.

"Including the floor!" Kaylee shouted.

Kaylee had spotted, even before Zachary, what lay before them: a long stretch of tube that was under construction. While the tops and side were built, the bottom was missing.

There was no turning back now, though, so they did the only thing they could. They leaned hard to the left and rode right up onto the wall. Zachary was coasting at a ninety-degree angle over a giant gap that dropped thousands of feet downward. A few loose serendibite fell from his pocket, tumbling into the abyss below.

Zachary peered over his shoulder and spied Quee, Skold, and Ryic making the same realization he and Kaylee had made moments before and adjusting their course accordingly. The first two Binary soldiers were chasing them, seemingly on autopilot, because they raced straight off the edge into the missing section of tunnel.

"Zachary, watch out!" Kaylee shouted. He had been so busy looking behind him that he didn't see what was coming up ahead. The wall from this portion of the tunnel was absent. Kaylee was now jetting along the roof.

Zachary spun upward. His speedwheels clung to the ceiling in a gravity-defying moment of exhilaration. He felt like he was going to throw up. Or was it down? He was losing all perspective on which way was which as he corkscrewed through the quickway tube.

A second wave of Binary soldiers had entered the tunnel, and these seemed to be learning from the others' mistakes, traversing the walls and ceiling just like Zachary and his gang.

Zachary's ears rattled as Quee's front speedwheel exploded right beside him. Without the forward drive of the motorized transport, Quee was losing traction on the wall.

"Help!" she screamed as her body slid toward the abyss.

Zachary reached out an arm, which was tricky because it took two to steer properly, and grabbed her ankle. Quee pulled herself onto Zachary, laying her chest flat against his back.

"Thanks," Quee said into his ear.

The tube dumped them back out onto the quickway, only the obelisk was much closer now. So close, in fact, that Zachary could see their sledge parked in the same spot beside it.

It would have been a straight shot if it weren't for the line of Binary robots standing with stun balls drawn.

"Cease now," one of them called out. "You are a danger to yourself and others. Organics are prohibited from using speedwheels."

Zachary blinked twice.

△ OBJECT: PATROBOT

LOCAL AUTHORITIES OF THE BINARY COLONIES, PROGRAMMED BY THE IPDL. THIS ROBOTIC POLICE FORCE IS UNWAVERING IN PURSUIT OF LAW AND ORDER. AVOIDS USE OF DEADLY FORCE IN FAVOR OF DETAINMENT.

Zachary turned back to see how close the pursuing Binary soldiers were, but was surprised to find that there was no sign of them.

"They're gone," Zachary said. "I don't understand. What happened to them?"

The others spun their heads for a look.

"There's a reason they're headquartered a hundred feet underground," Skold replied. "Obviously they want to stay off the patrobots' radar."

"Let's stop, then," Ryic said. "We've done nothing wrong. We can turn ourselves in. Ask for help."

"They'll detain and question us for hours," Skold replied. "We don't have that kind of time. Keep moving."

"We're armed with stun balls and will not hesitate to use them," a Binary patrobot warned the oncoming Starbounders.

Zachary didn't slow, and as a result a volley of stun balls came soaring toward him. He was able to dodge most, but one struck Quee, who was still piggybacking on top of him. She went rigid, her body freezing up immediately. If she hadn't been clinging to him, Zachary would have been the one sent into paralysis.

The barricade was just yards away. Zachary lowered his head and braced himself for impact. With tremendous force, he plowed right through the crowd of robots, sending them scattering like bowling pins. His companions knocked down the few left standing in his wake.

Nothing would keep them from reaching the sledge

now. All that was left was to figure out how to stop.

"One last question!" Zachary shouted. "How do you stop these things?"

"The robots return themselves to a standing position and glide to a stop," Skold said.

"Yeah, but our bodies don't rotate that way," Zachary called back.

"Which is exactly why they don't want flesh-and-bloods like you using these," Skold said.

The dead end was rapidly approaching.

"So, what do we do?" Kaylee asked.

"You let go," Skold replied, and he was the first to release his grip from the handwheel bar. As soon as he did, he went tumbling across the surface of the quickway. Zachary and the others had no time to contemplate a better solution. So they all opened their hands.

Zachary used the edge of his back speedwheel to decrease his velocity, but it didn't bring him to a full stop. He lost control and went rolling. It was still a painful crash. Zachary's face smacked against the ground and his legs went flying over his head. He could feel bruises forming with each successive bounce along the steel pathway.

Quee was tossed from his back.

He strained to sit up, and once he was certain that nothing was broken, he kicked his boots free from the footwheels and got to his feet. Skold, Kaylee, and Ryic were doing the same.

Quee lay limply on the ground.

Zachary and the others ran to her side.

"Quee? Are you okay?" Ryic asked.

But she remained motionless.

"Quee!" Zachary pleaded.

He looked back to see that the patrobots had picked themselves up and were charging toward them.

"Get her legs," Zachary said. "We'll have to carry her on board."

Kaylee grabbed her by the ankles and Zachary picked her up beneath her arms. The group ran for the entrance portal of the sledge. But Zachary's attention was on Quee.

"Guys," he said. "I don't think she's breathing."

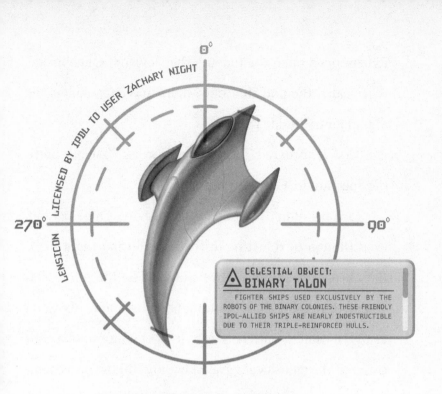

⚠ CELESTIAL OBJECT:
BINARY TALON

FIGHTER SHIPS USED EXCLUSIVELY BY THE
ROBOTS OF THE BINARY COLONIES. THESE FRIENDLY
IPDL-ALLIED SHIPS ARE NEARLY INDESTRUCTIBLE
DUE TO THEIR TRIPLE-REINFORCED HULLS.

«TWELVE»

"Let's put her in the hyperbolic pod," Zachary said. His heart was racing fast. Quee's life was in the balance and he knew time would be precious. He felt responsible. This had all been his idea. Quee had followed him, never questioning his leadership, just to prove she belonged as a Starbounder. And now she lay dying.

Zachary and Kaylee hurried through the main cabin to a clear plastic bubble with gray tubes snaking out from it.

Ryic popped open the top and they lowered Quee inside. Ryic sealed the pod shut once more and began adjusting digital levers beside it.

"Go," he ordered Zachary and Kaylee. "There's nothing you can do. Get us moving."

Zachary didn't like the idea of leaving Quee behind, even though he'd just be in the neighboring flight deck. But he also knew that Quee wouldn't be the only casualty if they didn't stop Commander Keel and his robot army. He waited until he saw billows of white smoke pour through the translucent gray tubes and fill the pod chamber, and then he left the main cabin.

Once he and Kaylee arrived in the flight deck, they buckled themselves into the pilot seats and activated the ship's starbox. Zachary looked out the front window and saw that the Binary patrobots had surrounded the sledge. They were swinging metal grappling hooks with magnetic claws at the outside of the ship.

"Those are density tethers," Kaylee said. "If they attach enough of them, we won't be able to take off."

A pair of the claws had already affixed themselves to the left side of the hull and more were being lobbed rapidly. Zachary tried to kickstart the sledge as fast as he could.

"You have already broken multiple protocols," one of the patrobots announced over the intercom. "Do not incur additional offenses. Unauthorized liftoff—"

Kaylee had flipped an off switch, shutting down any further communication from outside. Zachary could still see the patrobot waving his arms and demanding they stop.

"We keep this up, we're going to have a longer rap sheet than Skold," he said.

"Guess that's the price you pay for saving the outer-verse," Kaylee replied.

Zachary gestured his right hand slightly upward, engaging the sledge's thrusters, and rocked his left hand back and forth, shaking the ship's nose. The spacecraft lifted from the ground, but only a couple of feet, as the density tethers were holding strong.

"You need to give it a little more juice," Kaylee said.

Zachary clenched his fist and punched his arm in the air. With a burst of force, the ship jolted higher, but the tethers still wouldn't give. Only the right half of the vessel was rising. As the sledge continued to tilt, Zachary could hear Ryic and Skold go stumbling in the main cabin.

"What are you doing up there?" Ryic called out.

"Sorry," Zachary replied.

He twisted his wrist, causing the ship to spin in a rapid counterclockwise motion. Around and around it went, until the sledge finally broke free from the tethers with a loud snap and catapulted into the sky. Zachary had to react quickly to prevent the ship from colliding with the golden obelisk. He gestured frantically, straightening the nose and launching them through the clouds.

"Just keep us steady till we break out of orbit," Zachary said to Kaylee.

He unlatched his harness and ran back to the cabin, where Ryic was huddled over the hyperbolic pod.

"How is she?" Zachary asked.

"I've been trying to shock her system with adrenaline gas," Ryic replied. "She's breathing on her own, but hasn't regained consciousness."

"You know, we haven't exactly discussed what the plan is here," Skold said. "Let's say we do catch up with Keel and his army. Then what? We gonna take on a gizalith and a thousand Binary talon fighter ships from in here?"

"If we have to, yes," Zachary answered.

"You got some real brass on you, kid," Skold said. "But maybe you should take a look at what we're up against before you start making such bold promises."

Zachary followed Skold's eyeline through the door to the flight deck, and he could see the gizalith in the distance. To say it was massive wouldn't be doing it justice. It was gargantuan—it was almost impossible to comprehend how it was ever built in the first place. All around it were crescent-shaped ships that looked like bird talons, and together they were moving like a herd toward a galactic fold in the cosmos.

Zachary pulled himself back into the flight deck.

"Do you think we can catch them?" he asked Kaylee.

She checked the Kepler cartograph and made some calculations. "It's going to be tight."

The sledge continued to race forward. It was difficult to judge how much progress they were actually making, if any. But they must have been closing the gap, because the gizalith and surrounding ships were coming into clearer focus. As they did, Zachary could see that something was dragging behind the gizalith: an enormous funnel connected to three giant cylinders. Zachary blinked twice, hoping to identify the object, but all his lensicon could come up with was a heads-up display reading NO INFORMATION AVAILABLE.

"That's your star-killing device," said Skold, who had floated into the flight deck and was looking at the same thing Zachary was.

Of course. Those three cylinders were the perpetual energy generator that Skold had stolen from the Callisto Space Station. As for the funnel, Zachary guessed it was the kinetic force sink. The magnitude modulator must have been hidden inside.

"Kaylee, see if you can get us within range," Zachary said. "If we destroy that weapon, we don't have to worry about what the rest of Keel's plan is."

She was already pushing the sledge as fast as it could go. Zachary sat himself in front of the particle blaster controls. A glimmer of hope had appeared. Maybe all his worries would be for naught. Their ship seemed to be catching up. But the positive feelings vanished when two of the talons broke formation and started flying straight toward them.

"Don't engage," Zachary said. "Just try to get around them."

The talons weren't about to make that so easy. Whichever way Kaylee turned, the pair of fighter ships adjusted course to ensure an inevitable head-on confrontation.

"It looks like they want to crash into us," Kaylee said.

"They are robots," Skold replied. "Whether they're partially alive or not, if they're programmed to carry out an order, they never deviate."

Zachary began to fire at them, and while he was making direct hits, the particle blasts merely ricocheted off whatever protective metal the ships were made from.

With the talons forcing them into this dance of duck-and-dodge, the gizalith was getting away. And all Zachary, Kaylee, and Skold could do was watch. While Kaylee continued to maneuver the ship, seemingly at a stalemate, Zachary took a moment to focus his lensicon on one of the fighter ships.

Friendly? Clearly the outerverse database didn't get the memo about the Binary robots' rebellion.

"Those canisters attached to the sides aren't part of the standard model," Skold said. "They must have been custom-made."

Zachary scrolled down to the lensicon display's sub-heading entitled **SPECS**. A diagram appeared labeling every part of the fighter ship. Skold was right. There was nothing resembling the metal tanks hugging the exterior of the talons.

"What are they for?" Zachary asked.

"I don't know," Skold replied. "But it looks like they

had to remove some of the hull's reinforcements to attach them."

"A soft spot?" Zachary asked.

"It's worth a try," Skold said.

Zachary aimed the sledge's particle blaster at a canister hugging one of the ships. He fired, and when the projectile hit its target, the metal tank exploded, sending a gelatinous purple ooze spraying in an ever-expanding cloud into space. Moreover, Skold's theory was proven true, as the point of impact caused a chain reaction destroying the entire talon.

Zachary didn't hesitate, taking out the other Binary fighter ship the exact same way as the first. Kaylee flew the sledge directly through the cloud, which had now quadrupled in size due to the second talon's detonation, leaving a thin purple film on the flight deck windshield.

Zachary looked past the residue to see the gizalith and the herd of talons disappear through a galactic fold.

"If you hurry, we can still catch it," he called out to Kaylee.

She pointed the sledge toward the galactic fold. Zachary fidgeted nervously in his seat. He was tempted to push Kaylee out of the way and take over command of the ship himself, but he knew that he wouldn't be able to make it go any faster. After just a few short minutes—but what seemed like an eternity—they reached the edge of the galactic fold.

"When we get to the other side of this fold, our only objective is to take out the star-killer," Zachary said.

"We'll still be vastly outnumbered," Kaylee replied.

"Yeah, but at least now we know how to beat them," Zachary said.

The sledge flew through, and when they emerged in the distant galaxy, they were alone. The gizalith and the talons were nowhere to be seen.

"Where are they?" Zachary wondered. "How is that even possible?"

"Maybe they initiated their camouflage shields," Kaylee replied.

"No," Skold said. "Gizaliths are too big for any cloaking mechanism to work. They must have already jumped through another galactic fold."

Zachary was checking the Kepler cartograph for the

nearest fold, but instead of finding just one, three dozen appeared.

"It's a string nexus," Skold said, "where dozens of folds meet at one point."

"How do we know which one they went through?" Kaylee asked.

"We don't," Skold replied.

"If everything we've assumed up until now is correct, we know they're heading toward one of four suns," Zachary said. "We can start by checking if any of these holes lead directly to one of them."

It didn't take him long to cross-reference the Kepler cartograph with the location of the four suns.

"None of the systems can be reached in a single jump from here," he said.

"What about two?" Kaylee asked.

"There's hundreds of possibilities," Zachary replied. "And with three or more jumps, thousands." He clenched his fist and looked like he wanted to punch the holographic display. "We could really use Quee right now."

"Guys, get back here!" Ryic shouted from the main cabin.

Zachary detected a hint of panic in his voice. He flew out of his seat and exited the flight deck.

"What is it?" he asked. "Is Quee okay?"

"It's not her," Ryic replied. "There's a sound coming from the cryo freezer."

Zachary took a moment to listen and could hear it, too. There was rattling and banging, and it sounded violent. He immediately remembered the diamond-shaped creature pinned down to the metal table inside. But why was it suddenly acting up now?

Kaylee and Skold had both soared back into the main cabin to join the others.

"I think I know what's making all that noise," Zachary said. "There's some kind of crystalline creature in the freezer."

"Are you talking about that souvenir the Black Atom Society left for us?" Kaylee asked.

"Yep," Zachary replied. "And I didn't think it was very happy before."

"Let me go have a look," Skold said.

As the group moved toward the cryo freezer, Zachary heard not only the clatter but a vile screeching sound, as well. He was becoming less and less eager to have that door opened. But Skold was undeterred. He grabbed the metal handle of a nearby mag mop and gripped it like a combat stick. Then with his free hand he unlatched the freezer door and pulled it open to reveal the same creature Zachary had encountered during his dare. It was still pinned to the table, but its spindly legs were thrashing like mad in a desperate attempt to extricate itself. Skold choked up on the mag mop and was about to swing, but stopped himself when he realized that the creature was restrained.

"A scorpiosite," he said. "That's what you get when scorpiositic fever evolves. The question is, what's one doing on this ship?"

Opening the freezer door had only angered the creature further. In a moment of sudden fury, the virulent agent tore off its restrictive bindings and leaped from the table. Zachary tried to seal the freezer shut, but the scorpiosite had already made it halfway out, wedging itself between the door and the jamb. Skold tried to prod it back inside with the tip of the mag mop, but the virus squirmed its way through and attacked Zachary. The thin pincers at the end of its legs dug into his jumpsuit. He reached out to grab the creature's crystalline body and attempted to shove it off him. The scorpiosite didn't budge, though, its grip tightening. Skold swung at it with the mag mop, but the predator was relentless.

"Somebody get it off!" Zachary shouted.

Kaylee used her warp glove to punch at it, but that didn't help, either.

Zachary's eyes went wide in terror as he watched the base of the virus open up like a mouth and a syringelike appendage emerge. Now it was Zachary's turn to thrash. He could only imagine what would happen to him if he got infected.

Just then, Zachary heard a splintering, cracking sound. He looked down to see an ionic dagger embedded in the back of the scorpiosite. Then he glanced up to see who had thrown it: Quee. She was awake and floating five yards away. The creature released its grip and Skold swung the mag mop like a bat, slugging it back into the cryo freezer. Kaylee slammed the door shut.

The group let out a collective breath, but no one was more relieved than Zachary. All this time, he had convinced himself that he could face any obstacle on his own, but the truth was, there would always be something he didn't see coming. And that's what his friends were there for. That's why he needed to trust others to help him.

He touched the inch-deep pincer gashes left in his Starbounder jumpsuit and double-checked to see that his skin hadn't been cut. Between the photon blast hole in the suit's elbow and now this, he was going to need to see about getting a new one as soon as he got back to Indigo 8.

"Quee, you're okay," Ryic said, sounding beyond relieved.

"Yeah, and it looks like I woke up just in time," she replied.

"So, anyone want to tell me how a scorpiosite ended up on this ship?" Skold asked. "Come to think of it, *whose* ship are we on, anyway?"

"We stole it from the Black Atom Society," Kaylee replied.

"Maybe they were looking for a cure," Zachary added. "We walked past a research lab under category-one quarantine. Robots were experimenting on a family of cinderbeasts that seemed to be infected with some kind of disease. What if it was scorpiositic fever?"

"Did you say robots?" Ryic asked.

"That doesn't sound like a coincidence to me," Skold said.

"I want to know why that creature *just* lost it," Kaylee said. "It's been stuck in that freezer for as long as we've been on this ship, and it never made a sound until now."

"Something must have triggered it," Quee said.

"I didn't hear anything until right before we jumped through that last fold," Ryic said.

"That's when I blasted those two talons," Zachary said.

"So, what's the connection?" Skold asked. "It's not like the scorpiosite has any personal interest in the fate of two Binary robots."

"Well, nothing's changed on the inside of the ship," Zachary said.

"What about the outside?" Kaylee replied. "That purple sludge on the windshield have anything to do with it?"

Quee's interest was piqued and she floated up to the flight deck. The others followed behind.

"I know what this is," Quee said. "It's a pathogen attractor called bactobait. Tenretni authorities would use it on the bottom tier. They coated the streets with the stuff. All the airborne bacteria from above would flock to it so the rich people up high never got infections. Nobody seemed to care if the folks stuck on the lower levels got sick."

"Why was Commander Keel's army carrying giant canisters of it on their fighter ships?" Zachary asked.

"Apparently, to attract scorpiosites," Quee replied.

"How did they know there was one on our sledge?" Ryic asked.

"I don't think this has anything to do with our ship," Skold said. "What if they plan on using it to draw all the viruses out of the Olvang Nebula, and spread them across the entire cosmos?"

"First of all, there's no way they could get the scorpiosites past the electron fence," Zachary said. "And even if they did, they would wipe out every living thing in the outerverse."

"Exactly," Skold said. "Every *living* thing. They're robots."

Of course. The Binary robots that Zachary had seen

inside the Black Atom Society weren't looking for a cure. They were looking for a way to destroy all life. They were the traitors who were building the kinetic force sink on Luwidix. Olari just hadn't figured it out yet.

"So what does destroying suns have to do with the scorpiosite threat?" Ryic asked.

"Arbez, Lemeck, R-21, and Opus Verdana," Zachary said. "Any of them located in the Olvang Nebula?"

Kaylee began spinning the Kepler cartograph, then stopped on a holographic display and searched it. "No, not even close."

"Wait," Ryic said. "Right next to Opus Verdana, practically inside the sun itself, is a fold. I know of it only because they taught it to every Klenarogian in science class. It's completely unusable. Unless the sun wasn't there."

Kaylee had already adjusted the cartograph and was looking at a projection of the very fold Ryic was talking about.

"There it is," she said. "And it connects right back to the Olvang Nebula."

All the parts were falling into place. It was never about destroying suns. It was about spreading scorpiositic fever.

The Binary robots had built the device to eliminate Opus Verdana and create an unguarded exit for the virus. But first they had to test it on the similarly sized suns of Protos and Clu 5 to perfect it. Once the scorpiosites escaped, the talons would use the bactobait to lead them all across the outerverse. It was the perfect plan for sentient machines: unleashing a deadly plague that they were immune to.

"We need to get to that sun before Keel and his army do," Kaylee said.

"I know," Zachary said. "But I've finally realized something. We can't do it alone. We need to call for help."

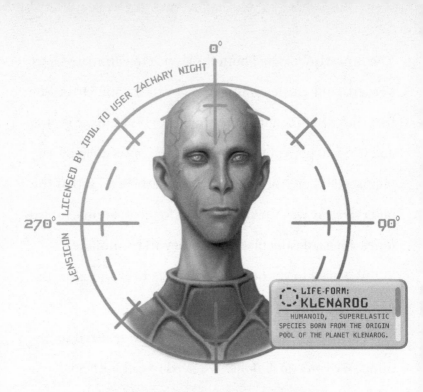

0°

270°

90°

LIFE-FORM:
KLENAROG

HUMANOID, SUPERELASTIC
SPECIES BORN FROM THE ORIGIN
POOL OF THE PLANET KLENAROG.

«THIRTEEN»

The sledge raced through fold after fold as it soared toward Opus Verdana. A grim cloud hung over everyone, most of all Ryic, whose home planet would be the first victim of the scorpiositic fever once its sun was extinguished. As Kaylee flew the ship, Zachary sat before the lang-link.

"I don't know when you'll receive this message, but it's urgent," he said. "We've learned of an imminent attack on

Klenarog's sun. Rebel Binary robots led by one known as Commander Keel are en route as I speak. Should they be successful in their attempt, we believe they plan on using a hidden galactic fold behind the sun to release the quarantined scorpiositic fever contained within the Olvang Nebula. Contact every Starbounder stationed within five folds of Klenarog to assist."

Zachary gestured toward a send command on the screen, then turned to the others.

"I've contacted every Indigo base in the outerverse," he said. "I also sent messages to Wayfare, even Captain Aggoman. I just don't know if anyone will receive them in time."

"I've been doing some analysis," Quee said from her seat on the flight deck. "I know you said you had some luck with those Binary talons, but I'm not sure we have enough firepower to take out the star-killer. The kinetic force sink will just absorb all the particle blasts."

"Klenarog will make any ship in its fleet available to us," Ryic said.

"We can't land and switch ships," Zachary said. "It'll be too late by then."

"Well, unless we come up with another plan, I say we hold tight until the cavalry rides in," Skold said. "I know you all have hero complexes, but me . . . I prefer living."

"I know a shortcut from here," Ryic said. "There's a fold that will take us into a starship hangar underground, just like the one at Indigo 8. There's no way the gizalith will make it through. It'll have to make two extra jumps. We'll beat it there by fifteen minutes."

"Lead the way," Kaylee said.

Ryic floated over and took the pilot seat from her. He buckled in and immediately deviated from the route on the Kepler cartograph. He was heading for a fold, and from the looks of the updated map, one that would take them directly to Klenarog. The sledge shot forward into the hole.

"I didn't think I'd be going home so soon," Ryic said. "And certainly not like this."

The ship emerged through the other side into a cavernous tunnel covered in moss and lichen. A trail of blinking green lights guided them toward an enormous domed hangar filled with starcraft that looked like pitchforks, except these had six prongs instead of three. A giant statue of a teenaged female Klenarogian, with scepter in hand and medallions hanging around her neck, towered in the center of the room. Uniformed Klenarogians, dressed in loose-fitting long-sleeved shirts and pants and armed with photon bows, were running up to the ship.

Once the sledge came to a stop, Zachary and the others unfastened their harnesses and got to their feet. Zachary instantly felt the effects of the planet's extra-heavy gravity. It was as if he had gained a hundred pounds, and even the smallest step was a struggle. Kaylee and Quee seemed to be having similar trouble. Skold less so. As for Ryic, he was completely at home. In fact, the awkwardness he usually carried himself with was gone.

Ryic exited the ship first, hands raised in the air.

"Don't fire," he said. "It's me, Ryic 1,174,831."

The Klenarogians all lowered their bows upon seeing him.

"Ryic 1,174,831," one of them said. "What are you doing here? You, who fled your destiny just before being anointed supreme commander?"

"Yes, it's true," Ryic replied. "I was afraid of being made anyone's leader. I could barely take care of myself. But these last few months have shown me that I'm capable—"

"Ryic," Zachary interrupted. "Not now."

"Right, sorry. I've come to ask for your help," he said to the uniformed Klenarogians standing before him. "We need a ship. Whatever's got the most firepower. Opus Verdana is in danger. It's going to be destroyed, just like the suns of Protos and Clu 5."

"Take anything you need," a Klenarogian called out. "We'll strap in and be right behind you."

Klenarogians started to run across the floor, while Ryic quickly surveyed the fleet. He eyed a bigger ship parked across the hangar. It was twice the size of a dread-nought, with debris cannons that appeared to be larger than the engines.

"We'll take the bison," Ryic said, eyeing the ship.

He headed straight for it, and Zachary and the others followed. They passed the large statue, where uniformed Klenarogians were bowing down at its marble feet before climbing aboard their pitchforks.

"And to think, those could have been my feet they were kissing," Ryic said.

One of the soldiers walked alongside him.

"Exactly what kind of threat are we up against, sir?" she asked.

As Ryic began to answer her, Zachary couldn't help but be amused upon hearing someone refer to his normally less-than-confident friend as "sir." But here on his home planet, Ryic acted differently, self-assured and bold. He wasn't just directing this one soldier, either. Others had gathered around him, and now Ryic was briefing the entire squadron on the specifics of their mission. They were nodding respectfully, and Zachary could see why Ryic had been chosen to be supreme commander.

The domed roof of the hangar began to open, revealing the red-tinged sky above them. As Ryic led his friends onto the bison, the first fleet of pitchforks took off, slowly rising through the hole in the ceiling. Once inside the enormous ship, Zachary and his companions passed through the main cabin.

"Skold, Kaylee, why don't you man those gunnery stations?" Ryic said, pointing to a pair of seats inside the turrets of the debris cannons. "Zachary, Quee, come with me."

He took them to the command deck, where a

Klenarogian soldier was already harnessed in before the control panel, making instrumentation checks.

"We're prepared for takeoff, captain," he said to Ryic.

Ryic gave a nod and buckled himself into one of the two pilot seats. Zachary sat in the other, while Quee brought up the Kepler cartograph. Ryic gestured for liftoff, and the bison soared upward, the deck window passing alongside the statue of the supreme commander—first her chest and neck, then the head, until the ship had departed the hangar.

Zachary got his first glimpse of the surface of Klenarog. It was covered in trees, although instead of a single trunk, each one had many, presumably to support the extra-heavy weight of the branches and leaves. Streams and rivers crisscrossed the land, and bridges connected the hundreds of thousands of tiny islands. Amphibious cars swam across channels and rolled over the islands, while large barrack-type buildings dotted the landscape. Zachary thought about all the people of Klenarog going about their business, not realizing that the sun above them could be extinguished at any moment.

The bison traveled higher, and soon the only thing

Zachary could see below was the lush green of the trees and vines blending together with the blue waters in a swirl. Gravity was beginning to weaken as well, and a moment before arriving in space, Zachary felt like he was back on Earth, no longer tugged down by the oppressive weight of Klenarog.

Just then, the command deck's video lang-link came alive and a face appeared. It was a girl who looked about the same age as Ryic, and on second glance Zachary realized she was identical to the figure depicted in the statue standing in the space hangar.

"Jengi 1,174,830," Ryic said. "I see they made you supreme commander in my place. Congratulations."

"Thank you," she replied. "I just received word from Fleet General Aria 1,613,552 that you'd returned. Of course, you have all our resources at your disposal."

"I've missed you, predecessor," Ryic said.

"And I you, successor," Jengi said. "Although this is not how I pictured our reunion. I thought I might be of some assistance."

"Unfortunately, there's little you can do from the Central Tower," Ryic said.

"Who said I was in the Central Tower?" Jengi asked.

The video lang-link adjusted to reveal that she was sitting in the pilot seat of a starcraft. A moment later, a golden pitchfork shot across the bison's bow, and Zachary could see Jengi saluting from the flight deck.

Ryic shook his head and smiled. "Good to have you back at my side."

As Zachary and Ryic guided their ship farther from the planet, it wasn't just Jengi backing them up, but close to fifty pitchforks piloted by Klenarogian soldiers. Opus Verdana was shining just a few million miles away, the circle of blinding white light too bright to look at.

"If the squadron can create a perimeter around the sun, the robots will have to blast their way through us first," Ryic said. "By then, hopefully, reinforcements will have arrived."

The bison and accompanying pitchforks raced through a thin asteroid field that encircled the sun. Once they reached the other side, Quee pointed toward the edge of a galactic fold opening between them and Opus Verdana.

"Look," she said. "The gizalith!"

The tip of the giant pyramid-shaped spacecraft was

emerging through the hole in the outerverse. The giza-lith pushed through, still carrying the star-killer behind it. What looked like a thousand Binary talons poured out from the fold as well. Either they didn't see the bison and pitchforks chasing toward them, or they didn't care, because their path never wavered from their target.

Commander Keel was leading his army straight for Klenarog's sun.

"You need to get a lot closer if we're going to have any chance of hitting them," Kaylee said over the flight deck intercom.

"Yeah, we're working on that," Zachary replied.

"Are these ships fast enough to catch up?" Quee asked the Klenarogian soldier manning the control panel.

"We could divert power from the camouflage shields and distortion sensors to the engine," he said. "Of course, that will leave us more vulnerable once we get there."

Zachary and Ryic shared a look. Sure, it would be risky, but what other options did they have?

"Do whatever you have to," Zachary said. "And tell those pitchforks to do the same."

The Klenarogian gestured to the control bay and

immediately the ship began to pick up speed. The distance between the trailing talons and the bison shrank.

"I've got one in my sights," Skold called out over the intercom.

But before he fired off a blast, Zachary watched as several Binary talons looped off course, which seemed to signal a third of Commander Keel's fleet to do an about-face. Soon, hundreds of talons had broken off from the herd and were now charging right at them.

"What now?" Kaylee asked from her gunnery station.

"Try to clear a path for us," Zachary said. "We have to get to the gizalith."

"Activate a mass lang-link," Ryic said to the Klenarogian soldier, who motioned a command to the control panel. Once the communication went live, Ryic continued, "Remember, aim for the metal canisters on the sides. That's their weak spot. Use your particle blasters, but save the full force of your debris cannons for the star-killer. That's the only target that matters."

The two opposing squadrons were on a collision course. Then a flurry of explosions ignited from both sides, and the bison flew directly into the fray. Kaylee and Skold were unloading cannon debris at any talon that crossed their path. Another enemy ship popped up in the bison's blind spot, but it was quickly blown out of space when a particle blast obliterated one of its canisters. Zachary glanced through the deck window to see that Jengi's golden pitchfork had delivered the killshot.

"She's always had a flair for the dramatic," Ryic said.

Zachary knew they didn't have time to dodge out of the way of every talon in their path, so instead he decided to plow through them. He pointed the nose of the bison forward and flew, battering the claw-shaped ships and leaving dented metal in its wake. Wave after wave of Binary robots continued to come at them. Ahead, the gizalith had slowed before Opus Verdana and begun rotating itself, aiming the star-killer at the sun's core. Now that they had flown closer, the shock of light emanating from the orb was so intense that if it hadn't been for the bison's thick, tinted windshield, everyone on board would have gone blind.

"We're never going to make it through," Ryic said over the mass lang-link. "There's too many of them."

"Well, maybe we can help even things out a little," a

synthesized voice replied. It wasn't a Klenarogian soldier. In fact, it sounded familiar to Zachary. Then a face appeared on the monitor. It was Captain Aggoman. "Usually I don't respond to distress calls from custodial runaways. But in this case, I figured I'd make an exception."

Then, out from the same fold that the gizalith and talons had exited, emerged Aggoman's starjunk, along with a fleet of Indigo 8 battle-axes following in tow. They flew into the heart of the firefight, shredding metal as they blasted their way through. And they didn't stop there, continuing to carve out a path for the bison as they raced closer to the gizalith.

Through the flight deck windshield, Zachary could see that the Binary mothership was in position, the starkiller charging but not yet activated.

"Kaylee, Skold, is the device within range?" Zachary asked over the intercom.

"Almost," Kaylee replied.

"My finger's itching," Skold added.

The gizalith turned its voltage rocket launchers in the direction of the approaching bison.

"This is why draining power from your ship's defenses

can be a very bad idea," the Klenarogian soldier said from the control panel.

The first rocket struck the outside of the bison, causing all the electronics inside to flicker.

"Fire back!" Zachary yelled over the intercom. A moment passed, but the ship's debris cannons remained idle. "What are you waiting for?"

"The voltage rockets must have shorted our entire weapons system," Kaylee replied. "It will take a minute to recharge."

"We don't have a minute," Zachary said.

He was right. The star-killer was starting to glow brighter.

"Send a mass lang-link to every pitchfork and battle-axe out here," Zachary said to Ryic. "We need all our firepower here right n—"

Zachary stopped midword, because the funnel at the end of the star-killer began to suck the energy out of Opus Verdana's core. The effects were rapidly apparent. The iridescent orb grew dimmer, and it started to shrink in size.

"Somebody, fire on that device now!" Zachary shouted.

Opus Verdana was becoming darker and smaller by

the second. Zachary could see that Ryic was watching the sun of his home planet die. And he could only imagine the panic and chaos that was surely overwhelming Klenarog and its people now.

A pair of Indigo 8 battle-axes emerged from the cluster of ships engaged in the firefight and swooped in, blasters a-blazing. But before either could lock in for a shot at the star-killer, they were both struck by voltage rockets. It seemed that each ship's steering lost power as they spiraled away from the target. A series of blasts from the gizalith's debris cannons finished the job, blowing them to space dust. Zachary winced, but had little time to mourn the loss of his fellow Starbounders.

"Kaylee . . . Skold?" Zachary asked.

"Still nothing," Kaylee replied.

Even if the bison's weapons did kick back in now, it would be too late. Opus Verdana had gone black. All that remained was a small, dense chunk of rock, completely drained of energy. What had been blindingly bright just moments earlier was plunged into total darkness. The one thing left shining in the outerverse was the gizalith. And suddenly it was moving, closer to the rock center of what was formerly Opus Verdana.

A grim expression overcame Ryic.

"How long before the temperatures plummet . . . and the entire planet freezes? Weeks? Days? Just hours? Until everyone and everything starves? Until nothing is left and Klenarog becomes a desolate, lifeless rock?"

"I don't blame you for being worried," Zachary said, "but if we're right about what's coming next, starving and freezing are the least of your planet's problems."

Zachary looked ahead as metal prongs extended from the tip of the gizalith and a galactic fold that had previously been hidden within the sun's corona opened. The hole widened and a hundred of Commander Keel's Binary talons flew through, disappearing from the space around Klenarog. Zachary moved in front of the mass lang-link.

"This is Zachary Night. All allied starships, prepare to fire on whatever comes out of that fold. I repeat, every particle blaster and debris cannon should be loaded and ready."

Only a handful of the pitchforks and battle-axes appeared capable of assisting, including Aggoman's star-junk and Jengi's golden ship, as the majority were still locked in an unrelenting exchange of fire with the mass of talons that hadn't departed through the hole. But those that did were flying into formation beside them, preparing to strike at anything that might come out.

They waited. Anxiously. What Zachary saw next left him as cold as the sun that had just been destroyed.

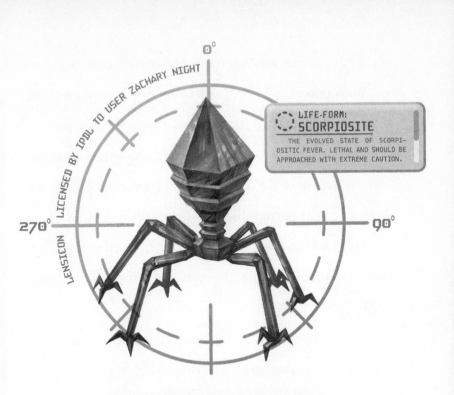

0°

270°

90°

LIFE-FORM:
SCORPIOSITE

THE EVOLVED STATE OF SCORPI-
OSITIC FEVER. LETHAL AND SHOULD BE
APPROACHED WITH EXTREME CAUTION.

«FOURTEEN»

Binary talons emerged from the galactic fold, but they weren't alone. Following close behind, lured by the bactobait stored in the canisters hugging the outside of the metallic ships, were whale-sized scorpiosites. Hundreds of them. The enormous, diamond-shaped creatures propelled themselves through space, leaving in their wake streams of liquid that immediately turned to ice.

"Fire!" Zachary shouted into the mass lang-link.

With power now restored to its debris cannons, the bison led its allies in a coordinated attack, pounding away at the talons and approaching virus. Aggoman's starjunk was the first to strike one of the scorpiosites, and Zachary watched as the particle blast shattered the creature's hardened crystalline exterior. Without its protective layer, the next round of fire tore through the scorpiosite's fleshy body, shredding it.

Other ships were having similar success, but for every one of the quarantined creatures that was destroyed, another ten slithered out from the fold.

Zachary saw that the talons were all flying in the same direction, leading the scorpiosites toward what appeared to be a specific destination. He turned to the Kepler cartograph, and sure enough they were heading straight for another galactic fold.

"What's on the other side of that fold?" Zachary asked.

"A string nexus," the Klenarogian solider replied.

"If the talons make it through with those scorpiosites, they'll spread to every corner of the outerverse," Zachary said. "And there's nothing anyone will be able to do to track them all down."

"Fortunately, the virus doesn't move as fast as starships do," Ryic said. "So they won't reach the fold for at least twenty minutes."

Kaylee and Skold continued to fire off debris cannons, but keeping the enemy onslaught at bay was proving increasingly difficult. The Binary robots had adapted their flight pattern, maneuvering the talons so that hitting the weak spot where the canisters were attached was nearly impossible.

"We know that Binary robots are programmed with orders," Quee said. "There must be a central hub for all communications on that gizalith. If we can get ourselves on board, I can hack in and reprogram those robots to fly back to the Olvang Nebula."

"And how do you plan on getting there?" Ryic asked.

Quee didn't have an answer, and Zachary was equally unsure. But it seemed like their only option.

"We're going to need every ship out here to cover for us," Zachary said into the mass lang-link. "And escorts on both sides until we arrive at the gizalith's docking portal."

Aggoman and Jengi were quick to respond, flanking

the bison on the tail and bow. Other volunteers encircled the rest of the ship. With the escorts firing from every side, the fleet made a collective charge for the gizalith. Zachary expected the Binary talons to swarm them, but the allied Starbounder spacecraft were being given a clear path to the giant floating pyramid.

"Proceed with caution," Zachary said. "I think they might be leading us into some kind of trap."

But his warning wouldn't help them, as a barrage of voltage rockets began raining down from the gizalith. As the bolts struck the surrounding escorts, one by one their power was shorted, and the disabled ships drifted aimlessly through space, leaving the bison exposed. Zachary calculated his chances. Make a final thrust for the docking portal, or fall back? More rockets were coming at them in a flurry, and he had no choice but to reverse course.

Once the bison had dipped clear of the gizalith's attack, it was immediately met by a threat even scarier than electron projectiles. A scorpiosite that had been trailing one of the talons was coming straight at them. It stretched out its long, spindly appendages and gripped down on the ship's metal exterior. Through the flight deck windshield,

Zachary could see part of the creature's body hugging the bison, but the rest of it was obscured.

"How do we get rid of that thing?" Ryic asked.

"Maybe we can use it to our advantage," Zachary replied.

He motioned his hand forward and the bison went flying toward the gizalith once more. And this time, he wasn't dodging the voltage rockets coming their way. The bolts were hitting the scorpiosite, but its crystalline armor was deflecting it.

"Not a bad shield," Zachary said.

There were smiles all around the flight deck—until a screeching sound reverberated from above and the scorpiosite's syringelike appendage punctured the metallic roof. The Klenarogian soldier unharnessed himself and reached into the nearest underbin, grabbing a photon bow. But before he could even turn and fire, six smaller scorpiosites—roughly the size of the one Zachary had found in the cryo freezer—squeezed out from the hole at the end of the appendage.

A particularly feral one wasted no time jumping onto the Klenarogian's chest. Its underbelly opened up and a thin needle shot out from it, stabbing the soldier in the neck. He let out a scream and dropped the photon bow, then clutched at the wound, desperately trying to stave off the infection. But it was futile. Black tendrils were rapidly spreading across his flesh, sucking the life out of him.

Zachary, Ryic, and Quee quickly put on their warp gloves. The other five scorpiosites were bouncing from wall to wall, no doubt looking for something to feed on. As Zachary reached his gloved hand into the underbin, he kicked one of the crystalline creatures away from him. The virus barely flinched, going after Ryic instead. Two others were flying toward Quee, propelling themselves with liquid blasts expelled from their tendrils. And the remaining two had set their sights on Zachary.

Zachary, now armed with a photon bow in his free hand, began taking shots at the scorpiosites. But just as the larger creature clinging to the outside of the bison was immune to the gizalith's voltage rocks, these smaller viruses seemed able to withstand the concentrated beams of superheated light. The blasts merely reverberated off their exoskeletons.

The same feral creature that had disposed of the

Klenarogian soldier leaped onto Ryic's back, and the thin needle protruding from its mouth was preparing to strike him next. With a thrust the needle shot toward Ryic's flesh, but it was stopped just an inch from his neck by a metal glove that clamped down and gripped it tight. The gloved hand snapped the needle clean out of the scorpiosite's underbelly. Zachary saw out of the corner of his eye that the glove belonged to Kaylee, who had floated into the flight deck's entryway. Skold was right beside her, with an ionic dagger in one hand and a sonic crossbow in the other. One of the viruses came at him and he stabbed it with the dagger. The blade managed to penetrate its crystalline shell, but just barely, and the creature was hardly deterred.

"Some things just don't like dying," Skold said.

"Then we need to get them off this ship," Zachary replied.

"I don't think they're going to crawl back up into that thing they came out of," Ryic said, gesturing to the giant syringelike appendage still sticking through the flight deck's roof.

"Yeah, I figured asking nicely wouldn't work very

well," Zachary said. "So I thought we'd throw them out. Spaceship walls are no obstacle for a warp glove."

"No way, I'm not grabbing one of those," Ryic said. "That thing just tried to turn me into a pin cushion."

Zachary wasn't asking. This was the plan. He rotated his wrist forty-five degrees and pointed his finger. A warp hole appeared before him and he stuck his glove through. A second hole materialized inches away from a scorpiosite. Despite its struggling, Zachary was able to grasp his fingers around its hardened exterior, and with a tug, he pulled it back to his side. The virus's pincer-tipped legs flailed wildly, but before they could clamp down on Zachary's arm, he opened another warp hole. Only this time the exit hole was on the outside of the ship, in the void of space. Zachary's gloved hand disappeared through the entry hole with the scorpiosite held tightly in the gauntlet, and once it emerged on the other side, he let go.

Zachary pulled his hand back through, and he watched out the windshield as the small organism drifted away. Kaylee and Quee disposed of another pair the same way, and Ryic begrudgingly did the same, although he made sure to go after the one whose needle-like appendage had already been removed.

With the remaining pair of scorpiosites eluding capture, Skold, who had no warp glove of his own, was left with a different job. He had removed the boots from the now lifeless and floating Klenarogian soldier and was cramming them into the hole at the end of the larger appendage to make sure that nothing else came through.

Finally Zachary managed to snatch one of the last two viruses, while Kaylee grabbed the other. Once he caught it, Zachary didn't have much trouble depositing the scorpiosite into space. Kaylee, however, had a real thrasher in hand, and the creature wasn't going quietly. It kicked and jabbed its spindly legs, and before Kaylee could yank it through the warp hole, the needle stabbed her arm. She was forced to let go, leaving Zachary to swoop in and finish the job. He clutched the organism and dumped it into the vacuum of space.

Kaylee was tending to her swollen limb, grimacing.

"Are you okay?" Ryic asked.

"I'm fine," Kaylee replied.

"We can't be sure," Skold said. "For all we know, you're infected, and scorpiositic fever spreads quick. We need to get you in quarantine, now. Along with the dead Klenarogian."

"Whoa, whoa, slow down," Zachary said. "Let's not overreact here. We don't know anything for sure."

"Exactly," Skold said.

"Better to be safe, right?" Ryic asked.

"That needle barely broke the surface of her skin," Quee said.

Zachary glanced over Kaylee's shoulder and could see a soft throbbing of black in her veins.

"Where should I go?" Kaylee asked.

"I saw some shipping containers in the cargo hold," Skold said. "Make yourself comfortable in one of those."

"That's ridiculous," Zachary said. "We need her up here, with us."

Skold ignored Zachary and gestured to the Klenarogian. "As for him, see if you can't shoot him out the vacuum tube."

"It's for everyone's safety," Kaylee said to Zachary.

She floated out of the flight deck and was gone.

"I'll take care of him," Quee said, pulling the floating body out back.

The enormous scorpiosite hugging the exterior of the bison was beginning to move its pincers again. And the appendage began to retract. Skold pushed himself toward it and wrapped his arms around the crystalline tube.

"What are you doing?" Ryic asked.

"What does it look like?" Skold shot back. "Once this thing leaves, we'll have a two-foot-wide hole in our roof. And no more oxygen."

In the midst of the flight deck infestation, Zachary had been too preoccupied to notice that the bison had never stopped moving toward the gizalith. Now it was just a short distance from the docking portal. But there was one last safeguard protecting the Binary mothership from being infiltrated—dozens of Binary robots with grappling hooks securing them to an outer deck rail, all armed with photon cannons.

"Even if we do make it, those robots will pick us off one by one before we ever make it across the O_2 bridge," Ryic said.

It was too late to turn around now. The talons and trailing scorpiosites were nearing the galactic fold to the string nexus. They had to get on that ship, even if it meant becoming target practice for a bunch of sniper bots.

Skold continued to wrestle the appendage, using all the carapace's strength to keep the tube from exiting the bison. The ship came into the docking portal and extended its O_2 bridge.

Zachary took one last look at the tethered robots, who all had their weapons pointed at the bridge.

"I'm not going to be able to hold this much longer anyway," Skold said.

"Then it looks like we're just going to have to take our chances," Zachary replied.

Just before he reached the tunnel extending from their ship's entrance portal, the sniper robots were gunned down in a spray of particle fire. Zachary stopped. He glanced out the glass window beside the bridge. There, behind them, was a sledge.

Suddenly a voice rang out over the lang-link.

"Excelsius would have been proud."

Zachary turned and floated back to the flight deck video monitor. There on the screen was Bedekken.

"I can't believe you're here!" Zachary exclaimed.

"You're clear to cross that bridge," Bedekken replied.

"We'll be covering your back."

Zachary nodded and started to push his way back to the tunnel.

"I told you, I can't hold this much longer," Skold said, still fighting off the large scorpiosite's appendage. "You need to get Kaylee a bio regulator. I'll stay back and see if I can't patch up the hole. If Quee's able to reverse the Binary order, we're still going to need a way home."

Zachary reached into a flight deck underbin and grabbed one of the bio regulators. He was about to take off again but stopped.

"You know, for someone who just wanted to clear his name, you've been awfully helpful," Zachary said.

"Yeah, well, if everyone in the outerverse is gone, there'll be nobody left to steal from."

Zachary gave him a nod and propelled himself forward into the main cabin. He continued toward the cargo hold, pulling himself along the wall. On the far side of the hold was a trio of shipping containers, only one of which was sealed shut. Zachary pried open the door and found Kaylee sitting in the corner, hugging her knees and clutching her arm, where the flesh was now blackening all the way to her fingertips.

"What are you doing here?" she asked.

"We may start losing air," Zachary replied. "And when we do, you're going to need this to breathe."

He tossed her the bio regulator, which floated into her waiting palm. Zachary eyed the black in her veins, which was stretching past her wrists.

"Don't look so glum," Kaylee said. "I'm sure you're probably worried about going in there without me, but you'll be fine."

Zachary shook his head. "I'm not as tough as you are. I think the only reason I've gotten us this far is because I've been trying to impress you."

"Tough?" She chuckled to herself. "A new shade of purple nail polish isn't the only thing that's changed about me since I got to Indigo 8. Back home, before I was Starbounder Kaylee, I was just Kaylee, a girl who slept with stuffed animals and kept the night-light on."

"Well, you fooled me," Zachary said.

"You should get going," Kaylee said. "Just shut the door on your way out."

"I hate leaving you like this."

"It beats getting blown out the ship's vacuum tube."

Zachary wanted to reach out his hand and give her one last comforting squeeze, but seeing as how she had been infected with the fever, that was a sure way to get it himself. So all he could do was smile, making his best effort to let her know that everything would be okay. But by the looks of her arm, he had his doubts. He locked the storage container's door back up and soared out of the cargo hold.

Ryic and Quee were waiting at the entrance of the O_2 bridge. Once Zachary arrived, the three began their crossing. Suddenly, more Binary snipers were emerging through slits in the gizalith, but before they could get any shots off, they were mowed down by the sledge still circling outside.

Zachary, Quee, and Ryic made it to the other side, and Quee used her cryptocard to hack into the entrance portal and force open the door. They were inside the gizalith. The three hurried through an atmospheric atrium and when they came out the other side, Zachary felt gravity pull him back to the ground. He looked around to see that the interior of the ship was an enormous open space encircled by hundreds of floors ascending to the top of the pyramid. Thousands of Binary soldiers moved busily throughout the different tiers, some on foot and some on speedwheels, and it was only a matter of time before the three young Starbounders would be discovered.

"Now how are we supposed to find that central communications hub?" Zachary asked.

"I've already uploaded the gizalith's floor plan," Quee replied, scrolling through her wrist tablet. "Finding it isn't what I'm worried about. It's getting there."

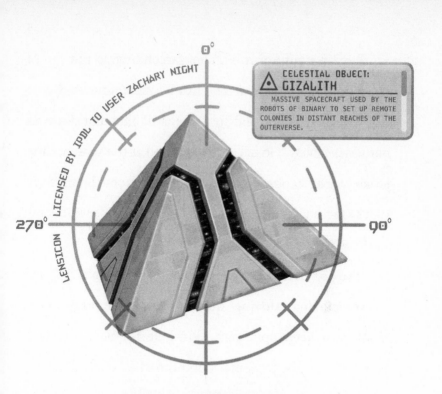

0°

270°

90°

CELESTIAL OBJECT:
GIZALITH

MASSIVE SPACECRAFT USED BY THE
ROBOTS OF BINARY TO SET UP REMOTE
COLONIES IN DISTANT REACHES OF THE
OUTERVERSE.

«FIFTEEN»

Zachary looked over Quee's shoulder at the blueprint
of the ship displayed on her tablet. He could see
that the central hub was located six floors up, on the
north end of the gizalith. It wasn't a terribly long distance
to travel, but how would they get past Commander Keel's
army of robots?

"Any air ducts lead up to that room?" Zachary asked
Quee.

She did a quick scroll on her tablet. "Afraid not."

"I don't suppose tiptoeing would work," Ryic said.

"Wait," Zachary said to Quee, still glancing down at her wrist tablet. "Go back." He pointed at the screen, then looked up at a room just down the hall from them. "Says that's where the ship's refinery is."

"So?" Quee asked.

"I've got an idea," Zachary said.

He started moving quickly, and Ryic and Quee hustled to keep up. They were able to reach the fuel depot without being spotted and the three ducked inside. Fortunately, there were no Binary soldiers stationed there, and Zachary's hunch was right. Just like at the refinery on the Mammoths of Xero, there were several robotic carriers—giant jellyfish-like porters with long mechanical tendrils snaking out from their clear bodies—hovering in a row.

"These should do the trick," Zachary said. "Quee, come with me. Ryic, follow behind us." Zachary approached one of the vehicles. "Porter, open storage hatch."

The jellyfish descended and its clear door lifted open. Ryic commanded a second carrier to do the same as

Zachary and Quee climbed aboard theirs. Once they were buckled in, Zachary said, "Exit to hallway."

The vehicle obeyed without hesitation, floating back into the pyramid's cavernous interior.

"There's a ramp to the left," Quee said, looking down at her tablet.

"Ninety degrees counterclockwise," Zachary directed the porter.

The hovering jellyfish moved effortlessly, and Zachary could see that Ryic's porter was right behind them. They were halfway to the ramp when Binary soldiers suddenly flooded the hallway in front of them, particle blasters in hand.

"Tendrils one, four, and six, strike approaching robots," Zachary instructed.

The carrier's mechanical arms lashed out, batting away the soldiers with brute force. They went flying over the edge of the balcony, tumbling toward the ground floor of the ship sixty floors below. A second wave of Binary robots charged at them, this time firing off beams of concentrated sound from their sonic crossbows, but they merely bounced off the vehicle's transparent shell.

"Tendrils two and three, disarm soldiers," Zachary said. "Tendril five, attack."

Two of the porter's mechanical arms snatched the crossbows from the robots' metallic hands and discarded them. Then tendril five swooped in like a wrecking ball, barreling through the soldiers in one fluid motion and knocking them thirty yards through the air. Hitting the far wall, the bots slid to the ground.

The two vehicles continued to ascend the ramp. From balconies above and across, more photon fire came flying at them. The glass outer shell of Zachary and Quee's porter was beginning to splinter under the constant barrage.

"The hub should be just on the other side of this next ring," Quee said.

As their carrier came to the junction point where they could either get off the ramp or keep going, Zachary gave a quick command: "Exit here."

The porter left the ramp and began moving around the ring toward the communication hub. Ryic, whose floating vehicle was traveling just behind, swung the porter's arms clumsily, dispatching several Binary soldiers barreling toward him on speedwheels. Before getting hit again, Zachary maneuvered his ride through the open door to the hub. It was a room filled with holographic displays that seemed to monitor all the vital functions of the gizalith. The far wall had thousands of screens that surveilled the visual feeds of every Binary robot in the giant pyramid and the ones piloting the talons outside.

"Stop and surrender," a Binary robot inside called out, with weapon drawn menacingly.

"Tendril two!" Zachary shouted.

The robotic jellyfish reached out one of its long arms and clamped down on the soldier's waist. It lifted him off his feet and flung him like a ragdoll, past Ryic's porter and over the balcony.

"Open hatch," Zachary said. The clear body of the vehicle split, allowing Quee and Zachary to drop to the floor.

Quee ran over to the far wall with the visual feeds of all the Binary robots and whipped out her cryptocard. She inserted the thin metal rectangle into a slot and began typing into her wrist tablet. Zachary came up behind her.

"Something's wrong," Quee said. "They built in a failsafe. A system defense that prevents remote override. And there's only one way to circumvent it. Commander Keel's unique Binary impression."

"What does that mean?" Zachary asked. "Do I need to get some kind of serial number or access code?"

"No. You need to get Keel's fingerprint," Quee said. "Or a whole finger. Whatever's easier."

"He could be anywhere on this ship," Zachary said.

"Not anywhere. Here." Quee pointed to one of the feeds that displayed a view of the gizalith's apex command center. "This is what Commander Keel is seeing right now."

"How do we know it's him?" Zachary asked.

"This series of ones and zeroes translates in Binary language to Keel's name," she said, gesturing to a row of numbers below the feed. "The apex is at the top of the pyramid. You have to get there soon. Look."

Quee pointed to another section of the wall where the feeds of the talon pilots were displayed. A group of them were rapidly approaching the galactic fold that led to the string nexus, with the scorpiosites following behind.

"We still have time, but not much," Quee said grimly. "I'll stay back and upload the override order so that it's ready to go once you bring back Keel's Binary impression. Ryic can cover me."

Zachary looked over to see that Ryic was still sitting in the jellyfish porter by the door, knocking back a handful of Binary soldiers that were attempting to enter. Zachary climbed back inside his own vehicle and sealed the fractured clear body around him.

He directed his robotic carrier out of the communications hub, past Ryic and onto the ringed platform of the 108th floor of the pyramid. He was about head back to the series of ramps leading upward but was surprised to find that there were now hundreds of Binary robots descending on him. It would be impossible to swat them all away, and even if he could have, Zachary knew that he wouldn't have time to make it to the top. At least not if he had to circle up the slowly rising ramps for another hundred floors. He needed a shortcut and fast.

He looked upward at the apex. What caught his eye was that the level directly above him—and every successive level—had a ringed platform identical to the one his porter was floating above right now. It reminded him of the geodesic dome jungle gyms he played on as a kid. It also gave him an idea. Back in the schoolyard, if some-one was strong enough, he would be able to climb up the inside of the dome to the top. Maybe his porter could do the same.

"Tendril one, two, and three. Grab the edge of the plat-form on the floor above." The mechanical arms reached upward and snagged the metal guardrail. "Pull."

The porter lifted itself higher into the air and was now dangling precariously over the thousand-foot drop.

"Tendrils four, five, six, and seven," Zachary said. "Grab the next platform and pull."

The carrier extended its tendrils to the next rail and vaulted itself two floors upward. Like a spider mon-key swinging from the branches of a tree or King Kong ascending the Empire State Building, Zachary's vehicle was rising up the middle of the giant pyramid on a direct path to the apex.

Keel's army of robots opened fire from each successive floor that Zachary passed, but the clear body of the jelly-fish was withstanding the assault. There was no telling how much longer it would hold, though.

The carrier made it all the way to the top, just one

floor beneath the apex. It flipped over the guardrail and ascended the final ramp. Once it reached the closed door to the command center, Zachary brought it to a stop.

"Open hatch," Zachary said. The clear body of the jellyfish split and Zachary dropped to the ground.

"Tendrils one through seven, smash down that door and enter."

The mechanical porter began pounding on the steel barrier, making huge dents until it blasted the door right off its hinges. The inside of the apex command looked like a smaller version of the gizalith, only its walls were all seethrough. There was a clear view of the outerverse from every side.

Zachary stood back and watched as photon cannon fire immediately bombarded the entering unmanned vehicle. The already splintered glass exterior exploded into pieces, sending shards flying everywhere.

"Tendrils, defend yourself!" Zachary shouted from his safe cover.

The robotic carrier's arms crushed the pair of soldiers standing guard at the door, but the porter wasn't able to move any farther as Commander Keel sent a rocket-propelled geigernade directly at it. The explosive detonated on impact, obliterating what was left of the jellyfish.

"Zachary Night, I know it's you!" Keel shouted through the door. "You're too late."

Zachary took out his warp glove and activated it. This had been his plan. To storm the apex command center and confront Commander Keel. But now that he was here, he wasn't entirely sure what to do next.

"The talons haven't reached the galactic fold yet," Zachary replied.

"I know the only way you can stop us is with my Binary impression," Keel said. The gizalith commander pulled out two more geigernades and squeezed his fingers around them. "But you're not going to get it."

Zachary opened a hole with his warp glove. As he stuck his arm through, another hole formed a few inches from Keel. Zachary reached through and swiped one of the explosive devices. He chucked it away from Keel to the far side of the room. Zachary's gloved hand went back for the other geigernade, but before he could grab it, it detonated.

Zachary pulled his hand back through the hole as the force of the blast blew Keel's hand to smithereens, tore the rest of his arm off, and sent him flying backward. The geigernade that Zachary had tossed exploded as well, but the damage was limited to a chunk of wall and a bay of computers.

In the chaos, Zachary grabbed a piece of broken glass from his destroyed jellyfish porter and charged into the room. Keel returned to his feet, but only briefly. Zachary slid across a battle strategy table and kicked him in the chest once he got to the other side.

Wielding the shard like an ionic dagger, Zachary slashed at Keel's body, leaving gashes in his copper exterior. Keel looked down at the mere scratches with a mocking sneer.

"You can't hurt me," Keel said. "Not like I can hurt you. Flesh is weak. A stew of water and carbon barely held together by ionic bonds. Metal is strong. A mesh of atoms so tightly woven that only the flames of a sun could melt it."

Keel stood up and thrust out his remaining hand, gripping Zachary's throat. He squeezed tight like a vise.

"We don't need to breathe like you," Keel said. "Blood doesn't flow through fragile tubes in our bodies."

Zachary was beginning to feel light-headed. He tried to fight back, but his arms were tingling, in danger of becoming unresponsive if he didn't do something quickly. Zachary eyed one of his porter's dismembered tendrils lying outside the door. Gathering his strength, he reached out with his warp glove and traded in the shard of glass in his hand for the mechanical arm.

Zachary swung it like a combat stick, a bigger, stronger combat stick than the one he'd become so adept at using back in the Qube on Indigo 8.

He flicked the flexible tendril and caused it to loop around the hand still clenching Zachary's jugular. With a tug he was able to pry Keel's fingers from his throat. He gasped for air, sucking in a lungful. Then Zachary took another swing. This time the metal tendril wrapped around Commander Keel's shoulder tightly.

Disarm and submit, Zachary thought.

And disarm he did. Zachary gave a mighty tug, and Keel's entire arm was ripped clear off.

Now for the *submit* part of the equation.

"Even for someone who doesn't feel pain, this is going to hurt."

Zachary grabbed a geigernade off Keel's waistbelt and shoved it in his hollow arm socket. He batted the robot back with the tendril, and with Keel's severed arm in hand ran for the door as fast as he could.

Zachary dove for cover as bits of Keel blew across the apex command center. Zachary picked himself up and kept running down the ramp toward the balcony of the 200th floor of the gizalith.

Without the floating jellyfish, climbing back down the center of the pyramid to Ryic and Quee would be impossible. The ramps would take too long even if they weren't swarming with blaster-wielding robots. At least, they would on foot. Zachary glanced to a rack on the nearby wall where speedwheels hung on hooks. He strapped Keel's arm across the back of his Starbounder jumpsuit, then grabbed a pair of wheels and tossed them to the ground. As he stepped his friction boots inside, the latches snapped into place. He reached for one of the barbells and took hold. Once he lowered it to the ground, he was propelled forward, gaining momentum with every second. The downward trajectory of the spiraling ramp only added velocity.

An onslaught of Binary soldiers were soon blocking his path, but Zachary lowered his head and slalomed around them. He never slowed. He was rocketing straight for the next wave of Keel's army, but these soldiers were firing. Fortunately, the combination of going fast and staying low to the ground made him an almost impossible target to strike.

The farther he descended, the faster the loops became. It was a head-numbing blur. Round and round he went, zipping past what seemed like an endless cavalry of metal. Finally he was approaching the 108th floor, and there was that tiny little detail about not being able to stop. So Zachary simply let go. Instead of using his own hands to slow down, he pulled Keel's arm from his back and jammed it against the ground. There was a shower of sparks before he gradually came to a stop.

Zachary disconnected the speedwheels from his boots and ran for the communications hub. Ryic was still guarding the door inside his robotic jellyfish while Quee waited by the far wall.

"Thank goodness!" Quee exclaimed upon seeing Zachary. "The talons have nearly reached the fold."

Zachary passed her Keel's arm and collapsed to his knees after he did.

Quee immediately pressed the hand up to a sensor built into the wall. Binary numbers began to blink across the visual feeds as Keel's unique impression was verified.

"We're in," Quee said. It took only a few seconds before she was stepping back. "The order has been approved. They're turning around. It's over. And nobody can reprogram them again without this." She set Keel's arm down on the ground. "Ryic, if you'd do the honors."

"With pleasure," Ryic replied. "Porter, crush that hand."

One of the mechanical tendrils made a fist and came swinging down like a sledgehammer, smashing the metallic appendage to bits.

On the visual feeds Zachary could see that the Binary talons had turned around and were now heading for the fold that would lead the scorpiosites back to the Olvang Nebula.

Even though he was already weightless, Zachary

instantly felt lighter. And it wasn't just because he had saved the outerverse again. He had done it with his friends, and a whole lot of others at his side. Of course, they weren't done yet. They were still on a hostile ship and needed to get back to the bison. Ryic lowered his carrier and opened the clear body, allowing Quee and Zachary to enter.

"Return to the entrance portal on refinery level," Ryic commanded the jellyfish.

The vehicle took off, and for the six floors down the ramp, the Binary soldiers stepped aside and gave the carrier clear passage.

"I didn't just reprogram those talon pilots," Quee said. "I reversed all of Keel's orders. The IPDL will be able to take it from here."

They reached the atmospheric atrium connected to the O_2 bridge and exited the jellyfish. As the three crossed back through the clear tube, Zachary watched as talons zoomed past the gizalith and toward the fold, with the oversized scorpiosites following in their wake. Zachary, Ryic, and Quee reentered the bison, and once inside, they found that Skold had successfully repaired the hole left by the scorpiositic virus.

"This ship ready to fly?" Zachary asked.

"Good as new," Skold replied. "I see you guys took care of business on your end, too."

"You check on Kaylee?" Zachary asked.

"She doesn't look so good," Skold answered. "I think we should head for the nearest medical freighter. Make sure she gets looked at ASAP."

Zachary was already floating for the flight deck control panel. He retracted the O_2 bridge and initiated the ship's engines.

"Buckle up, everybody," he said.

Just then, out from the nearby galactic fold emerged a scorpiosite larger than any of the previous ones. It rivaled the gizalith itself in size and seemed completely disinterested in following the bactobait of the talons.

"What the heck is that thing?" Ryic asked.

"The mother virus that all the others spawned from," Skold replied.

Zachary was trying to turn the bison away, accelerating

the ship in the opposite direction from the massive virus. But before they were able to break free, one of the scorpiosite's clawed appendages pinched down on the hull, gripping it tightly. Everyone inside the flight deck was thrown forward.

"A little help here," Zachary called into the mass lang-link.

The sledge, pitchforks, and battle-axes made a unified attack on the beast, but their collective firepower wasn't enough to destroy it.

"These starcraft are built to fight other ships," Jengi replied over the lang-link. "Not scorpiosites."

The virus was hooking another pincher into the outside of the bison, and it was starting to drag the ship toward its opening stomach cavity. It didn't seem like there was anything anybody could do to stop it. Until an enormous static harpoon pierced the underbelly of the mama scorpiosite, sending shockwaves through the creature that not only caused it to release its grip, but sent it fleeing for the hole to the Olvang Nebula.

Zachary and his companions weren't sure where the attack had come from. But then they watched as a ship turned off its camouflage shield and revealed a familiar skipjack. Wayfare appeared on the video lang-link.

"Even better than a terra whale," he said, grinning from ear to ear. Wayfare's ship followed the space virus toward the hole. "But there's no victory unless I can hang it on my wall."

The skipjack flew off, and it didn't look like there would be any more surprises for the Starbounders between here and the next fold.

In the distance, Zachary could see hundreds of IPDL relief ships flying toward Klenarog. The people on Ryic's home planet would be safe. Now he just hoped the same could be said for Kaylee.

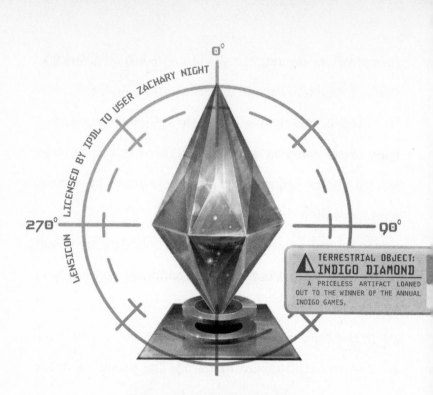

0°

270°

90°

⚠ TERRESTRIAL OBJECT:
INDIGO DIAMOND
A PRICELESS ARTIFACT LOANED
OUT TO THE WINNER OF THE ANNUAL
INDIGO GAMES.

«SIXTEEN»

Zachary stood next to Ryic on the long, sand-covered field of Indigo 3, host of this year's annual Indigo Starbounder Games. All the SQs from each camp were lined up for the opening ceremony, with their selected captains and co-captains standing at the front. A procession of unusually tall, crimson humanoids native to the host planet rode atop the backs of large rock creatures, carrying colorful streamers that danced in the wind.

Apollo whispered back to his fellow Lightwings, "We're going to destroy these other camps."

Zachary might not have shared his cabinmate's aggressive rallying tactics, but it didn't matter. He was just happy the only destruction that was going to take place would be out on the field.

He looked at all his fellow Starbounders lined up beside him, and for the first time realized they were just as capable of saving the outerverse as he was. They just hadn't had the chance yet.

Zachary glanced across to where the Lightwing girls were standing. He looked past their captains and found Quee in back, right beside Kaylee. After escaping from the mama scorpiosite, Zachary had guided the bison directly to a medical freighter floating through the Tranquil Galaxies. By the time they'd reached it, Kaylee's arm had been infected all the way to her elbow, and the IPDL surgeons on board were forced to amputate it before the scorpiositic fever spread to any vital organs. She'd been given a robotic prosthetic in return, one that was indistinguishable from her real arm, sort of like Skold's carapace.

Zachary gave her a nod, and Kaylee waved back

with her new fingers. A group of trainees from Indigo 3 marched out playing twisty wooden instruments that resembled rainsticks and theremins, emitting eerie sounds that seemed more suited to an old black-and-white science fiction movie than real life. But this was their idea of entertainment. As the performance continued, Henry Madsen walked up behind Zachary and Ryic.

"Gentlemen, I hope you're enjoying the ceremony."

"It's not going to last much longer, is it?" Zachary asked.

"Oh, I'd get comfortable if I were you," Madsen replied. "Hey, either of you seen Skold since the show started?"

Before Kaylee was even out of surgery, Skold had had Zachary negotiate the outerverse pardon they had promised him, exonerating him from all his previous crimes. And Madsen was the IPDL official who had signed off on it. With his name cleared, Skold had been invited back to Indigo 8 as a visiting instructor to teach diplomatic protocol and hot-wiring abandoned starcraft (although that would be offered as an elective only). He had joined the rest of the base at the Indigo Games, but now seemed to have gone missing.

"No, we thought he was with you and the other resident advisors," Zachary said.

"Last I saw, he was getting ready to turn in our official rosters, but that was half an hour ago," Madsen said.

Zachary and Ryic shrugged, and Madsen started walking. Then he stopped and turned back.

"I almost forgot why I came to see you in the first place," he said. "When I arrived, this was handed to me by Indigo 3's director. She said I should give it to you." Madsen pulled out an envelope with Zachary's name written on it from his pocket. "The strange thing is that she said they've been holding on to it for sixty-five years, with specific instructions to wait until you were here personally to receive it."

Zachary took the envelope curiously, but before he could open it, the music ended with a crescendo and one of the crimson humanoids jumped down from his rock creature and approached a tall glass podium. Behind him stood a pedestal draped with silk, hiding something beneath it. He spoke in his native tongue, but speakers around the sandy field translated it into different languages for each Indigo camp, depending on where they were standing.

"Welcome, fellow Starbounders!" Everyone cheered. "For the next five days, you will test your strength and agility, your brains and problem-solving skills, in both team and individual events against your rival Indigo bases. Points will be tallied, and only one camp will emerge as the victor. And until next year's Games, it will hold on to the prestigious prize that commemorates what it has accomplished: the one and only Indigo Diamond!"

The humanoid pulled the cloth from the pedestal to reveal absolutely nothing. There were gasps of confusion from the crowd. But Zachary and Ryic exchanged knowing looks. In unison they said, "Skold."

"If this is a prank, it's not funny," the crimson figure said. "The Games will not commence until the trophy is returned."

The opening ceremony came to an abrupt halt, and the SQs were quickly intermingling, chatting among themselves. The Indigo 8 Lightwing boys and girls gathered, allowing Zachary and Ryic to meet up with Kaylee and Quee.

Kaylee took one look at them. "What is it?" she asked.

"You mean, *who*?" Zachary said.

"I'll give you one guess," Ryic added.

Just then, a pitchfork zipped by overhead and disappeared into the clouds. All four of them watched, and none seemed too surprised.

Zachary looked down at the envelope that was still waiting in his hand. He used his fingernail to open it. Inside was a pair of dog tags on a chain with the name IO MECH inscribed on them, along with a typed letter. He read it to himself.

I know what you've just been through, and I know it probably seems impossible to believe that the outerverse could be in jeopardy again. But it very much is. You need to go to the Galactic Bank. A safety deposit box will be waiting there in your name, and only your retinal scan will open it. The rest of your instructions will be there. Zachary, this matter is of utmost importance. The future and the past depend on it.

Yours truly,

Io Mech

°°-°-293---°

Zachary stood there, rereading the letter. Why was he receiving mail from the greatest Starbounder who ever lived? Someone who disappeared decades before he was even born? There had to be some mistake.

"Zachary?" Kaylee asked. "You okay?"

Zachary folded the letter back into the envelope with the dog tags and shoved it into his pocket. Then he looked up at his friends.

"Any of you know where we can steal a ship around here?"

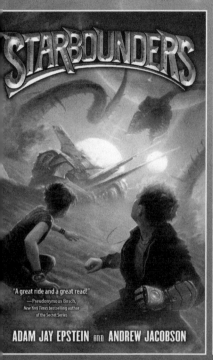